TABBY
Under the TREE

TABBY Under the TREE

Ben M. Baglio

Illustrations by Ann Baum

**Cover illustration by
Mary Ann Lasher**

SCHOLASTIC INC.

New York Toronto London Auckland Sydney
Mexico City New Delhi Hong Kong Buenos Aires

ISBN-13: 978-0-439-02532-4
ISBN-10: 0-439-02532-X

12 11 10 9 8 7 6 5 4 3 2 1   7 8 9 10 11 12/0

Printed in the U.S.A.   40
First Scholastic printing, November 2007

Special thanks to Ingrid Maitland

One

"Mandy! Where *are* you?"

Mandy Hope heard her grandmother's voice floating up the stairs to the bathroom where she was brushing her teeth. There was a tide of foamy toothpaste on her upper lip, like a mustache. It was early — not yet nine o'clock on a frosty Saturday morning.

Still sleepy, Mandy wondered if she'd made plans she'd forgotten about. Her feet were freezing, but there wasn't time to find a pair of clean, warm socks in her messy bedroom. She took the stairs two at a time, leaping down into the hall and startling her grandmother with a bear hug from behind.

1

"OK, I'm here!" she announced.

"Well," said Dorothy Hope with a twinkle in her blue eyes, "it's the first day of December." She linked arms with Mandy and led her toward the kitchen. Mandy smiled at her grandfather, who was seated at the kitchen table, a mug of tea and a flat, brown paper package in front of him.

"Hi, Grandpa," she said.

"Morning, sweetheart."

Mandy's father, Dr. Adam Hope, was buttering a slice of toast and humming a Christmas carol. "Ouch!" he said, dropping the toast back onto the plate. "That's hot. Morning, Mandy."

"Hi, Dad. Where's Mom?" Mandy asked.

"She's in surgery," her father replied. "Mrs. Harris shut the car door on her collie's tail."

"Oh, no! Poor Bailey!" said Mandy. "Is he going to be OK?"

"Yes. Luckily, it's not too serious," said Dr. Adam, ladling a spoonful of raspberry jam onto his toast. "But sore, I imagine, poor guy."

Mandy knew Bailey was in very good hands. Both her parents were veterinarians. Their modern clinic, Animal Ark, was attached to the family's old stone cottage in Welford, one of the prettiest villages in the Yorkshire area of England.

Mandy sat down beside her grandfather. Winter sunbeams pooled on the scrubbed pine table, slanting in through the kitchen window. There was a fat redbreasted robin on a branch outside. The kitchen at Animal Ark was always cheery, but with Christmas approaching, it seemed even cheerier.

"Mandy, dear," said her grandfather. "Do you know what day it is today?"

"I've already reminded her," Mandy's grandmother said, leaning over to give the package a nudge.

"It's December first," said Mandy. "I don't see why . . . Wow! Is that package for me?"

"Yes," said her grandmother. "And I'm dying for you to open it. Go on!"

Mandy sat down and began pulling up the tape. "Great! I love surprises. Thank you!"

"What's that?" said a voice, and Mandy looked up to see her best friend, James Hunter, in the doorway, his Labrador retriever, Blackie, beside him.

"Hi, James," Mandy said. "It's a gift from Gran and Grandpa."

"Come in, James," Gran said, smiling. "I'll pop a slice of bread in the toaster for you."

Blackie broke free and burst in, then put his front paws up on the table to peer at what Mandy had in her hands.

"Down!" Dr. Adam groaned. "Blackie, your paws are *filthy*."

"Sorry," said James, grabbing hold of Blackie's collar and hauling him away.

Mandy gently extracted a sheet of thin poster board from the wrapping. It was a beautifully painted scene of rolling, snow-covered hills dotted with trees and stone walls, just like the view from Mandy's bedroom window. There were twenty-four little doors cut into the poster board, all closed, with numbers on them. "It's an Advent calendar! Wow! What a gorgeous one. Thank you!"

Mandy held up the calendar for her father, grandmother, grandfather, and James to see.

"Thank you!" Mandy smiled.

"I found it in a store in Walton," Dorothy Hope said. "I thought you'd like it, sweetie. It really is beautiful, isn't it?"

Mandy looked down at the calendar again. It didn't just look like the view from her window — it *was* the view from her window! "Look, James," she said. "We've walked here with Blackie."

"You're right!" said James. He leaned over and pointed. "That's Axwith Tor above Hart's Leap Ranch."

"And there's High Cross Farm and Welford Hall," Mandy added.

The calendar's doors were scattered across the landscape, some set among the branches of an oak tree, cleverly camouflaged among the knotted whorls of wood, some in a sky streaked with woolly clouds, others dotted across an open field.

"The store owner said it had been painted by a local artist," said Tom Hope.

James touched the bottom right hand corner of the work. "Here's a name."

"Matilda Richards," read Dr. Adam. "Hmm, I don't know the name, do you, Mom?"

"Can't say it rings a bell," said Gran. "But she can certainly paint!"

"Can I open a door now?" Mandy asked, running her fingers over the tiny cutouts.

Her grandmother nodded. Mandy carefully pried open the first of the doors. A cute gray squirrel peered out from among the pine needles of a snow-covered branch, its cheeks stuffed with a tasty kernel. Its fur had been so skillfully done with delicate blue-gray brushstrokes, it almost seemed alive.

"It's so sweet!" Mandy said in delight. She stood up. "I'll hang it right here on the door of the cereal cupboard so I don't forget to open any of the doors."

"OK," said Dr. Adam, rinsing his plate at the sink. "I'm off to give your mom a hand next door."

Mandy's grandfather shrugged on his coat. "We're off, too. We've got some Christmas shopping to get done."

"What are you two up to today?" Gran asked, bending to pick up her shopping basket.

"We're making wild-bird treats," James told her. "We've found this awesome recipe on the Internet for suet balls."

"Have fun!" called Gran, waving as she stepped out of the kitchen door. A blast of cold air entered the kitchen.

"Brrr!" Mandy said. She finished clearing the table so they had plenty of space to work in, then turned expectantly to James. "Did you bring the yogurt containers?"

James fished in the big pockets of his jacket. "Eight total," he announced, bringing out the stack of small plastic pots with a flourish. "Added to yours, that makes sixteen."

"Great." Mandy collected the other things they needed from the pantry and lined them up next to the stove.

James put the empty yogurt cups on the table and started to read aloud from the recipe: "Cut the lollipop sticks so they are the same length as the base of the container."

Mandy handed him a pair of scissors, and James snipped efficiently at the sticks until he had a small pile.

"Tie a medium-long piece of string to each of the lollipop sticks," he went on.

Mandy looked inside a drawer for a ball of string. "I'm not sure we're going to have enough string. . . ."

"Well, we'll see," James said. "I'll cut up pieces of string while you start melting the lard."

"OK," Mandy agreed. She unwrapped the lard and dropped it into the saucepan.

"Ugh!" James commented, coming over to look in. "It doesn't smell very good."

"That's because you're not a *bird*! Anyway, it's not finished yet," she said, stirring the greasy white goo.

When the lard had transformed into a simmering, clear liquid, Mandy turned off the stove and left it to cool. "Now," she said, feeling businesslike, "let's finish the containers." She sat down beside James at the table. "But this is the end of the string!" she announced, snipping it into two pieces.

James surveyed the row of plastic tubs, each with a shortened lollipop stick beside it. "We'll have to go to the post office. That's not a bad thing," he added. "Blackie hasn't had much of a walk today and he's full of energy."

As soon as Blackie heard the word *walk*, his ears shot up and he barked, tail wagging joyfully.

"Lucky for you, Blackie!" Mandy said, tugging a thick pair of socks out of her boots and wriggling into them.

James wrapped a woolly scarf around his neck and pulled on his gloves. "I'm telling you, it's freezing out there," he said.

"Well, we'll run!" Mandy suggested, slipping her feet into her boots. "Come on!"

*   *   *

Mrs. McFarlane, the postmistress, jumped when James and Mandy came bursting in through the door.

"I won!" Mandy said, gasping. "My hand touched the door before yours!"

"You two are in high spirits today," Mrs. McFarlane remarked, with a smile. She stood on tiptoes to look out of the window. "That poor dog looks worn out. What have you done to him, James?"

"Oh, he needed to burn some energy," James assured her. Outside, Blackie's breath was like smoke in the crisp air. His leash, tied to a railing, was pulled tight as he strained to keep an eye on where James had gone. "Wow! It's boiling in here."

"I have the heat turned up high," Mrs. McFarlane said. "And you're dressed for the Arctic. Take off some of those woolly things you're wearing."

Mandy got down to business. "We need a ball of string, please. We're making wild bird treats and —"

She turned around as the bell on the door tinkled, and a boy about her age stepped inside. Mandy didn't know him, so she smiled at him in a friendly way. His jeans were very loose, pooling around his boots and touching the floor at the back. His pale face was framed by the black hood of his sweatshirt and tufts of spiky blond hair stuck out around the edges. He didn't smile back.

"Hello," Mrs. McFarlane said pleasantly. "Can I help you?"

The boy ignored Mandy and James, though James was sizing him up rather obviously. "Um, yeah," he said. "My dad wants the newspaper delivered."

Mrs. McFarlane reached under the counter for a small book. "No problem," she said. "What's your address?"

"It's . . . uh . . . Step-up Cottage," he answered.

"Hi there," Mandy said cheerfully. "Did you just move here?"

"Yeah," he said, looking at his boots. "From Manchester." Manchester was a large city on the other side of England, about eighty miles from York. Mandy could detect a northwest accent in his voice.

"Name?" Mrs. McFarlane asked, her stubby pencil poised.

"Skilton. My dad's David, I'm Wayne," he said.

"You'll like it here," Mandy told him. "Welford is great."

"Don't think so." Wayne shook his head. "There are only cows and sheep and miles of nothing."

Mandy looked at James, and he raised his eyebrows at her.

"It is a little different from a city like Manchester," James admitted.

"There's a skee ball evening coming up at the Fox and

Goose," Mrs. McFarlane piped up. "That might be fun. You'd meet some of the locals, David," she added helpfully.

"Wayne," said the boy. "I'm Wayne — and um . . . I'm not interested in skee ball. Did you get the address?"

"Step-up Cottage," Mrs. McFarlane repeated. "*Walton Gazette*, right?"

Wayne shrugged. "I guess so." He yanked open the door of the post office, stopping in the doorway to tie his shoelace. The cold swirled inside.

Mandy pulled her hat down over her ears. "Thanks for the string, Mrs. McFarlane." She and James headed outside, stepping awkwardly around Wayne.

Blackie strained forward to greet them, trying to lick Mandy's hands while James untangled him from the post. Suddenly, he spotted Wayne coming out of the post office. He sprang forward, tugging the leash out of James's hands.

"Blackie, *wait*!" James pleaded.

Blackie bounded up the steps, barking a noisy welcome. Wayne frowned and backed away. He ducked under the railing and jumped off the steps, then walked away without saying a word.

"What's *his* problem?" Mandy exclaimed. Blackie's tail stopped wagging, and she stroked his soft black head. "Poor boy!"

"Blackie only wanted to say hello," James said. "Maybe he doesn't like dogs."

"Maybe. But he didn't exactly seem pleased to meet us, either," said Mandy. "I guess that's one neighbor who won't become a friend!"

Two

"His name is Wayne," Mandy told her father, snapping a lollipop stick in half.

"Wayne Stilton," said James. He was jamming a stick into a yogurt container. "Like that cheese."

"It's *Skilton*; it has nothing to do with cheese," Mandy corrected him.

"If they've got pets I'm sure we'll see them at Animal Ark," said Dr. Adam.

"I don't think there are any pets in the family," Mandy said, remembering Wayne's odd reaction to Blackie. She went over to stir the bird-treat mixture, which had been left to cool on a high shelf so that Blackie couldn't reach it. It was stiff and gooey now that sunflower seeds, raisins, bread crumbs, and peanuts had been added to the melted lard.

"It smells quite yummy," Mandy said as James held his yogurt cup out to be filled. "We'll have more than we need for our yards," she went on. "We could take a few over to Mr. and Mrs. Hardy at the Fox and Goose; then, customers at the restaurant could watch the birds, too."

"Good idea," James said.

"Have fun," said Dr. Adam, stepping over the dozing Blackie on his way out of the kitchen. "I'll see you later."

Mandy continued spooning the mixture into the yogurt cups, while James held the strings that were tied to the stick in the base of each pot. Mandy stepped back to admire them, all packed with nourishing ingredients and ready to hang.

"Come on," she said to James, and Blackie jumped up at once. "Let's go and see the Hardys."

Mandy walked carefully over the icy ground, carrying four yogurt containers in a small open box. The bird treats were not yet completely cold, and the mixture trembled as she walked. As they approached the Fox and Goose, she spotted Sara Hardy under the eaves of the thatched front porch. She was carrying a box, too, though it looked heavier than Mandy's.

"Julian!" Mrs. Hardy called. "Open up!"

James sprang to take the box from her. "Hello, Mrs. Hardy."

"Oh, James! How gallant you are. Julian's indoors somewhere, digging out last year's Christmas ornaments." She nodded toward the box James held. "I've been in the garage looking for the tree lights. Hello, Mandy. What have you got there?"

"Hi, Mrs. Hardy. James and I have made some treats for the wild birds. We thought you might like to hang them in your yard."

"Thank you! What a great idea," Mrs. Hardy said, opening the door. "Come inside. Have you had lunch? I made some sandwiches earlier."

"Now *that's* a great idea!" James said with a laugh, setting the box of lights down on a table.

Mandy liked being inside the Fox and Goose. It was dim and cozy with uneven stone floors and a log fire that was always ablaze and crackling in the colder months. The smell of good food hung in the air. As there was nobody around at this hour, Mandy put the box of bird treats on the countertop.

"What a lovely tree!" she said, admiring the big, fresh pine tree standing in a paper-covered base. The branches dipped beneath the weight of tiny snowmen, twirls of colored tinsel, glistening gold pinecones, and plump red Santas with crooked hats.

"John decorated it," Mrs. Hardy explained. "He came home early because his school was being used to film a movie." John Hardy was Sara Hardy's stepson; he was James's age, and even though he lived in Welford only during school vacations, they were all good friends. Sara passed around a platter of crusty white-bread sandwiches, oozing with mustard and mayonnaise. "Those are not for you, Mandy," she added, pointing to some of the sandwiches. "They've got meat in them."

Mandy chose a cucumber-and-cheese sandwich. "Yum, thanks."

James was already biting into a second sandwich.

"Why don't you go and find John when you're finished?" Sara suggested. "He'll be outside with the rabbits, I suppose. The Fox and Goose hotel for bunnies is very full just now! You can leave Blackie with me."

"OK," Mandy said. "Thanks for the sandwich, Mrs. Hardy."

James took yet another sandwich in his fingers and passed the plate to Mandy, who helped herself to a second one. They stepped out into the walled yard behind the main eating area. A hazy cover of gray mist hung in wisps in the crisp air.

"John must be in the shed," Mandy guessed, since there was no sign of the short, dark-haired boy in the yard.

John Hardy had been crazy about rabbits ever since he'd chosen to study them for a school project. He had two of his own, named Brandy and Bertie, and he looked after Imogen Parker Smythe's pet rabbits when she was on vacation, which was fairly often.

"Imogen's got four rabbits, doesn't she?" James recalled. "That makes six in total. It must keep him really busy."

"Seven," Mandy corrected him. "Button's baby, Bubbles, is staying here over Christmas break. My mom told me. John doesn't think of it as work, really. I don't think there's anything he'd rather be doing."

Just then, John appeared at the door of the shed with a rabbit tucked in his arms. He kept the rabbit hutches in the outbuilding so they would be warm in winter and safe overnight. John's bunnies also had the option of a large, enclosed outdoor run with portable shelters in case of rain.

"Hi, John!" Mandy called, going over.

"Hello, you two," he said. His nose was red, and his

dark curls were flattened onto his forehead by the wool hat he wore.

"Did you have a good semester?" James asked.

"Not too bad," John replied. "Look! Hasn't Bubbles grown?" He held out the rabbit in his hands.

Mandy ran her hand up the rabbit's long, velvety ears. "Hello, Bubbles," she murmured. The little rabbit belonged to a family who lived in Walton, which meant that Mandy didn't get to see her very often, so she was especially glad that John would be taking care of her for Christmas vacation. Bubbles twitched her little nose and let Mandy rub gently between her ears.

"I'm taking them all outside," John said. "It's cold, but they need to run around in the fresh air for a while."

"Is that Brandy?" James asked, pointing at a large, russet-colored rabbit hopping around in the run. John nodded. James went on. "And that one is . . . wait, don't tell me. . . ." A rabbit with one straight and one droopy ear was grooming himself busily in a patch of sunlight.

"That's Imogen's Bob," John filled in.

"Gosh!" Mandy exclaimed, as another rabbit popped out of a shelter and sniffed at the dewy grass. "Bertie's put on some weight, John. He looks a lot bigger than when I last saw him."

"He's an amazing eater," John admitted. "Also, I left

half a box of cookies out here yesterday and I think he ate all of them."

"Uh-oh!" Mandy knew that rabbits loved sweet treats but that they were not very good for them.

"Not sick, so far," John added.

Mandy admired the hard work John had done to make sure the rabbits had plenty of space to move around in. She hated to see rabbits, who were sociable animals and loved to run and dig, confined in hutches for twenty-four hours a day. She watched as John lowered Bubbles into the run. The rabbit happily kicked up her back legs and hopped away to join her friends.

"One more to go," John said, turning back toward the shed. Mandy and James followed. Dust from the rabbits' bedding danced in the light streaming through the window.

"Where does Bubbles sleep?" Mandy asked, looking at the row of hutches.

"She's in with her mom, Button." John was sliding the bolt on a sturdy hutch that had been built, Mandy knew, with help from retired carpenter Ernie Bell. "Hello, Button," he said. He scooped her up and headed out to the run once more, struggling to hold the cute brown rabbit, who seemed eager to get down. "Whoa!" he said.

Mandy smiled as Button shot out of his arms and began racing around in happy circles.

"All out!" John declared with satisfaction, dusting himself down. "Hey, are you coming to the skee ball night next week? It's to raise money for a charity called Birds of a Feather, which helps injured wild birds. It should be fun."

"Not everybody thinks so!" James said, making a face.

John looked surprised. "What do you mean?"

Mandy remembered Wayne's dismissive remark. "Oh, it's just that there's a new boy in the village. James and I met him at the post office this morning. He seems really annoyed to be living in the country, and he thinks skee ball is *boring*."

"Oh well, we can't please everyone," John said philosophically. "Here, have a look at this." He took a notebook out of his pocket.

Mandy looked over John's shoulder. "What is it?" she asked.

"Well," John began, sounding a bit shy, "I've been designing an obstacle course for the rabbits. People don't realize how bored rabbits can get and that they really enjoy solving problems. So I've designed a series of challenges for them."

"What a great idea!" Mandy said. She'd seen rabbits pushing on doors that opened outward and pulling with their teeth on doors opening inward as if they'd watched people using doors and figured out which way the hinges worked. "You're right. They are smart and they love to have something to do."

"Do *they* like skee ball?" James joked, and John pretended to sock him.

"Very funny!" he said. "Now, look here. I've got a network of tunnels, ramps, and openings for them to explore, with lots of toys everywhere. It's going to be like an adventure playground when it's finished."

"Wow," said Mandy, looking at the drawings John had made. There were right-angled turns in long, hollow tubes, some propped on ramps to take the rabbits uphill, then plunge them down a slope and pop them out onto what looked like a sandbox.

"Never mind the rabbits." James pushed his glasses higher up on his nose. "*I'd* like to play in it!"

Inside the run, Bubbles was digging, scraping the earth with her front feet. A shower of grass landed on her face and she shook her head. It flew off in all directions.

Mandy grinned. "She's demonstrating her intelligence!"

Bubbles shook her head again, and her long ears wobbled. She looked up at Mandy, then dipped her head and began to groom.

"Let's go in and have a hot drink," John suggested.

"OK," Mandy agreed, though she really wished she could get inside the run and spend more time with the rabbits.

They walked toward the back door. "When are you going to start building the obstacle course?" James asked.

"I'm still getting all the materials together," John said. "I've got a couple of plastic drainage pipes from a friend of Dad's, and I cut a door in the side of a big wooden tool chest, so that's a start. I want to finish it before next semester begins."

"We'll help," Mandy offered, as John pulled open the door.

"Thanks!" he said.

The warm interior of the Fox and Goose had Mandy quickly stripping off her hat and gloves again. Julian Hardy was halfway up a stepladder, draping a twisted green wire studded with tiny glass bulbs around the walls. Mrs. Hardy was handing him tacks, Blackie at her feet. Mr. Hardy hammered the tacks, and a picture on a hook wobbled.

"Careful," warned Mrs. Hardy.

"Hello, Mr. Hardy," Mandy called.

"Mandy, James, thanks for the bird treats. They look good enough to eat!" he said.

"Finished!" Mrs. Hardy announced when the end of

the lights were in place. "Let's see if they work, OK? Flick the switch, John!"

Mr. Hardy came down from the ladder, and John went over to the plug in the wall.

"Ready?"

"Ready!" everyone chorused.

The small glass bulbs came alive, casting a rainbow of blue, green, and red around the room.

Mrs. Hardy smiled. "Good work, Julian."

"They look great, Mr. Hardy," Mandy agreed. Now it really felt as if Christmas were just around the corner!

"Are you coming back to Animal Ark?" Mandy asked James as they walked across the village green.

"Can't," James replied. "We're putting up *our* Christmas tree this afternoon."

"Lucky you!" said Mandy. "We don't have one yet."

She waved to Mrs. Ponsonby, passing by at a snail's pace in her ancient car, and called hello to Walter Pickard, who was walking on the opposite side of the street. It was great living in a place where you knew everyone. *Almost* everyone, she corrected herself, wondering if they'd ever meet the rest of Wayne's family.

"Oh, James, look!"

Up ahead, sitting in a pale pool of wintry sunlight, was a cat. It was a dark, stripy-gold color, with black-tipped ears and white paws. One snow-white front paw was lifted to its mouth. The cat licked it delicately, then rubbed its face, eyes closed. A plump, gold tail was curled around its body like a sumptuous scarf.

"What a gorgeous cat!" Mandy said softly, halting James in mid-stride with her hand. "Don't frighten it away."

The cat stopped washing and looked up at James and Mandy. It sat still, examining them with interest. It twitched slightly when Blackie snuffled, but it didn't run away.

"I wonder who it belongs to?" Mandy whispered.

"I don't know," said James. "I've never seen it before. It's really pretty, isn't it?"

"Beautiful," Mandy agreed quietly. She wanted to pet it to see if the striking tabby fur was as soft and thick as it looked from a distance. She took a step closer, and the cat stood up and backed away, a wary expression on its face.

"Hello," Mandy said softly. She sank to her knees and held out a hand.

But the tabby didn't want to make friends. It turned away and squeezed through a narrow, vertical gap in a wooden fence, leaving the sidewalk empty once more.

Three

Mandy ran over and crouched down to the spot where the tabby cat had squeezed through the fence. Through it she saw a stretch of dull brown grass and the trunks of a few bleak-looking trees.

"It's gone!" she exclaimed, as James came up.

He shook his head. "Can't we go in? Isn't there a gate?"

Mandy walked along the fence and pushed at a pair of high-paneled gates, but they were locked. "Well, we don't want to trespass, anyway," she said. "I guess we'd better leave it. . . ."

She was about to turn away, wishing she could have

one more glimpse of the beautiful cat, when she heard a strange murmuring sound. James heard it, too. He looked at Mandy, frowning. "What's that?"

It was coming from right behind the fence. Mandy ducked down and crept back to the gap. She put her eye to the opening, motioning to James. He squeezed up beside her to look.

The cat had reappeared — and this time it had been joined by a pair of baggy blue jeans and big black boots. *There's something familiar about those slouchy jeans,* Mandy thought. They were Wayne's jeans!

Just then, Wayne knelt down and ran his fingers over the cat's soft, golden coat. "You're such a good boy," he told the cat. "Yes, you are. Are you hungry? Should I bring you a treat?"

"Well!" Mandy quietly let out the breath she had been holding.

"It's that Stilton boy!" James said, nudging Mandy aside for a better view.

"Shh!" she said. "Don't let him hear us! He might think we're spying on him."

"We're not," James reasoned, stepping back. "We just happened to be passing by."

Mandy stood up and brushed the dirt off her knees. "So, he has a cat," she said. "A really beautiful golden tabby cat. Who would have guessed?"

"From the way he acted," James recalled, "you would have thought he hated animals. I guess you can never be sure about people."

"Well, I'm glad the cat has an owner," Mandy said. "And Wayne really seems to love his pet."

Blackie whined, as though he'd gotten impatient with hanging around in the cold, looking through fences.

"Oh, Blackie, shush!" James chided. "Mandy, we'd better go."

"Yes," Mandy agreed, reluctant to be spotted by Wayne, who was even less likely to be friendly if he thought they were following him. "I just hope this isn't the last time we see that gorgeous cat."

Mandy finished her homework in front of the log fire in the living room at Animal Ark. She was flushed from a hot bath and full from her mom's vegetarian lasagna.

"A golden tabby, did you say?" Dr. Emily Hope looked at Mandy over the top of her book.

"Yes. It was a sort of stripy gold, dark in places, with huge white feet," Mandy said. "Gorgeous."

"The golden tabby is usually a type of the Persian cat," her mom explained.

"Did it have the characteristic snub nose of the Persian cat and a thick, bushy tail?" asked Dr. Adam.

"A very bushy tail," Mandy said. "But he's slender and

has delicate features. He didn't look like the Persian cats I've seen."

"Maybe it's just his unusual coloring that's a throw-back to his Persian ancestry," Dr. Emily remarked. "Anyway, tabby tiger cats, as some people call them, are quite rare."

"That's right," Dr. Adam agreed, removing his slippers to toast his toes by the fire. "The unusual golden color is caused by a recessive gene that's now only found in captive tigers. Pretty amazing, isn't it? Golden tabby tiger cats tend to be larger than other domestic breeds and, because of the effect of this recessive gene on the hair shaft, they have softer fur than their ordinary orange relatives."

"Gosh," Mandy said. "I didn't get near enough to pet him. I wish I had."

"I'm sure the boy — Wayne, is it? — or his parents, will bring him in for a checkup at some point," Dr. Emily said.

"I hope so," Mandy said, yawning. She closed her textbook with a snap. "I'm tired. And the sooner I go to sleep, the sooner morning will come and I can open another door in my Advent calendar!"

"This looks just like Bubbles!" Mandy ran her finger over the tiny painting behind the open door. It showed two wild brown rabbits in the middle of a snowy field. The artist had perfectly captured a rabbit's endearing inquisitiveness. Sitting up on its hind legs, the bunny in the picture stared at Mandy with dark brown eyes, looking alert and curious.

Mandy hung the calendar back on the handle of the cupboard. The little door she had opened that morning was marked with the number 8.

"How're the rabbits over at the Hardys'?" asked Dr. Adam as he stacked the dishwasher with the breakfast plates.

"John's busy giving them lots of fun things to do," Mandy replied. "James and I are going over there today —"

She was interrupted by a volley of barking outside the kitchen door.

Mandy's dad grinned. "This must be James now." He flung open the door.

"Can you *believe* it!" James exploded, holding on to the door frame with both hands. He sounded so indignant, Mandy burst out laughing. Then she noticed that, below the hem of his coat, he was soaked from the knees down. Blackie, who stood beside him, his tail drooping, stepped inside the kitchen and shook himself, scattering droplets of muddy water in all directions.

"Oh, no!" Mandy moaned. "I just earned my allowance mopping this floor!"

"Sorry," James said huffily. "It's that boy. That Stilton boy . . ."

"*Skilton*," Mandy corrected.

"Well, *him*," James growled, still hovering in the door.

"Take off your shoes and come in," Mandy instructed. "You might as well. I can clean up again if you drip. What happened?"

Dr. Adam snatched up the clean white coat he wore for the clinic and gave James a consoling pat on the head as he went past. "Your Saturday can only get better, James. . . ." He chuckled.

James raised a hand in farewell and went on talking. "I was coming along to meet you and *he* went by on a bike at top speed, right through a huge puddle, and splashed me! I'm sure he did it on purpose." He took the small towel Mandy offered him. She found another towel under the sink and began to rub Blackie down.

"He certainly doesn't seem to want to make friends," Mandy said. Blackie stretched up and licked her face.

"He's mean," James said, dabbing furiously at his pants with the towel.

"Never mind about him," Mandy advised. "I'll just get

the mop and clean up in here, and then we'll go and see John's rabbits."

"OK," said James, polishing his glasses and no longer frowning. "It's the day they're decorating the tree on the village green, don't forget. I don't want to miss that."

"We won't," Mandy said.

"I hope Wayne won't be there," James added. "On the green, I mean."

Mandy smoothed the fur on Blackie's head. It was still damp. "He probably won't come," she said. "You know, he may be very kind to his cat, but he should be careful not to make enemies of his two-legged neighbors!"

John Hardy was using a small rake to clean out the shelters in the rabbit run. The rabbits were sitting around in groups, watching him. Only Bubbles sat apart, Mandy noticed. She fished in her coat pocket for a bunch of parsley and some carrot tops.

"Can we help?" she asked.

"Thanks," John said. "I need to put all of this dirty straw into those garbage bags and haul it to the compost pile. Here, I'll give you each a pair of disposable gloves." As he reached into his plastic tray of cleaning equipment, he wobbled and put his hand to his head.

"Are you feeling OK?" asked Mandy.

"Not really," John replied. "I'm sort of dizzy."

"Well, let us do the hard work," James said. He took off his mittens and pushed his hands into the stretchy gloves.

"Can I get in with the rabbits and hand out a few treats first?" said Mandy.

John nodded. "Sure."

"Why is Bubbles sitting alone?" Mandy asked, walking slowly toward the rabbit.

"She's been a little quiet today," John said. "I don't know why."

Mandy crouched down beside Bubbles and put a gentle hand on her back. Bubbles turned around to sniff at the treats Mandy held. Waving a fresh green carrot top, Mandy expected the rabbit would show some enthusiasm, but Bubbles just turned away again.

"Not hungry, little one?" Mandy murmured. The other rabbits bounded over, putting their cold paws into Mandy's lap and making her laugh as they reached up to touch their soft noses to her face. Barney seized several stalks of parsley and zigzagged away with it, glancing back over his shoulder with a catch-me-if-you-can look to the others.

"Everybody's feeling frisky today," James observed.

"Not everyone." Mandy tried to stroke Bubbles again, but she hopped just out of reach.

"She's a little grumpy," John said. "Maybe Barney makes her feel uneasy. He's very dominant, though he hasn't been unfriendly to Bubbles. Better to leave her alone for right now. Come and give me a hand with this."

Reluctantly, Mandy got up and left Bubbles. It was unlike her to be disinterested in a visitor or a treat. Mandy felt uneasy about it as she hauled the bulging bags of straw to a heap in the yard. On the return trip to the rabbit run, she smiled when she saw Brandy and Bob chasing each other in a large, hollow cement pipe John had put in the run. They darted in and out, around and around, kicking up their hind legs. Then Bob joined in, racing after the others; suddenly, he stopped dead and made a vertical leap to turn all the way around in midair!

"That's what they do when they're really happy," John said, and Mandy heard a note of pride in his voice.

She decided not to say anything about her concern over Bubbles; she knew he loved rabbits more than anything else in the world, and if there was something seriously wrong with Bubbles, she was sure he'd be the first to notice.

They worked on the run until Julian Hardy called to them from the back door of the Fox and Goose. "There's

quite a crowd on the green now," he said. "Are you coming to help decorate the tree?"

"Be there in a minute," John called back.

He was transferring the rabbits, one by one, to the indoor hutches. It was getting dark, and colder, too, and Mandy hurried to finish laying down fresh straw for their bedding while James filled their water bowls. Then she carried Bubbles to the hutch she shared with Button and put her inside. The rabbit shook her head, making her ears tremble, before tucking her front paws under her chest and closing her eyes.

"I'll come and see you tomorrow," Mandy promised.

She hurried to catch up with John and James as they headed around the front of the restaurant, making for the village green.

Mandy smiled when she caught sight of Blackie weaving in and out of the gathering crowd. Sara Hardy had threaded a festive scrap of silver tinsel through his collar. Everywhere Blackie went he was petted by villagers who recognized him; in the end, James called him over and clipped on his leash to keep him out of the way.

"Show off!" James said playfully, rubbing Blackie's glossy black head.

The sky was heavy with clouds, and the air was

bitingly cold. In the center of the green stood the huge fir, its branches shivering in the wind.

"I hope it snows," Mandy said, scanning the sky. "It would be fantastic to have a white Christmas."

"Oh, I hope *not!*" said Mrs. Ponsonby, overhearing her. She hitched her Pekingese dog, Pandora, higher under her arm. "Pandora doesn't like snow!"

Mandy smiled. Pandora was wearing a little tartan coat. "Well, you look lovely and cozy in that outfit," she said, stroking the little dog's head.

It was good to live in a village like Welford, Mandy thought, like being a part of a very large family. Welford wasn't as bad as Wayne Skilton thought, at all!

Mrs. Hardy passed out steaming mugs of homemade soup. Julian was at the top of a ladder resting against the fir tree, fiddling with an electrical cable. Ernie Bell stood below, calling up advice.

"Keep it steady, now," Mr. Hardy warned Mr. Pickard, who was holding on to the base.

Mandy spotted her mother talking to Jean Knox. She went over. "Hello, Mom, hi, Jean. Where's Dad?"

"He's doing something mysterious in the kitchen," Dr. Emily replied.

Mandy wrinkled her nose. "Like what?"

Her mom smiled. "He won't say."

At that moment, Dr. Adam came striding across the green toward them. He was shrouded in a heavy coat and woolly hat, and his beard glinted with beads of frost. In his hands he held a large oval platter, covered over with aluminum foil.

"What have you got there?" Dr. Emily asked.

"It's my contribution to the tree-decorating ceremony," Dr. Adam announced, unpeeling the foil. "The best mince pies you'll taste anywhere!"

"Those look like the mince pies of a very accomplished cook!" said Mandy's grandmother.

Mandy took a bite of hers. "Hmmm, they *are* good, Dad."

"Thank you," he said, as he headed off with his platter. "Mince pies!" he called. "Come and get them while they're warm."

Mandy finished her pie and then, inspired by her beautiful calendar, which, so far, had celebrated nature's own decorations, she strung the lower boughs of the tree with loops of shiny blackberries and twigs of holly. She had wanted to hang the remaining bird treats she and James had made, but her mother had talked her out of it.

"It'll only encourage the wild birds to a tree that isn't very safe for them to sit in," she explained. "Not while it's covered in electric lights."

"Time for the countdown!" Julian Hardy shouted. "Who wants to turn on the lights?"

"Let Dr. Adam do it," Mrs. Hardy called. "In return for the wonderful mince pies!"

The crowd hushed and John took up the count: "Ten . . . nine . . . eight . . ." he began, and the voices around him swelled in volume until everyone roared out "one!" Dr. Adam flicked the switch. The tree came alive with color, bringing a chorus of "ahs!"

"It's gorgeous!" Mandy exclaimed.

"Merry Christmas, everyone!" Dr. Adam called.

Mandy took a few steps back to admire the tree. Welford Green looked like a picture on a Christmas card; all that was missing was a dusting of snow. But the lovely scene was slightly spoiled by the sight of litter — a discarded potato chip bag and a single plastic shopping bag. As she bent to pick it up, she saw something moving at the bottom of the tree.

In the half light, with the branches moving slowly in the breeze, Mandy couldn't make out what it was. A bird, or had one of John's rabbits escaped? Then she heard the softest of meows. Just a small, trilling sound — but she knew it was the sound of an unhappy cat.

Mandy dropped to her knees and crawled under the

drooping branches. Wayne's beautiful tabby looked back at her from where he crouched behind the trunk.

A glow from a bulb in the branch outlined his large ears and striking head in eerie blue light.

"Hello, beautiful!" Mandy murmured. "What are you doing here?"

The tabby shifted farther into the light, and Mandy realized that only one of his eyes was open. He lifted a paw and rubbed the closed eye, then looked at Mandy and meowed again. The lower rim of his eye was red and swollen, and the thick, gold fur on his cheek was flattened by moisture streaming like tears from underneath the eyelid.

"You're hurt!" Mandy breathed. "Oh, poor cat. What happened to you?"

Four

Mandy brushed a knot of pine needles out of her hair. "James!" she called. "Wayne's cat is under the tree. He's hurt!"

James ran over. "Hurt?" he echoed in alarm. "Hurt how?"

"There's something wrong with his left eye," Mandy explained. "He can't even open it. Will you get my parents?"

"Your dad went back to Animal Ark to get some more mince pies," James said. "I'll go find your mom."

Mandy crawled back under the tree. It felt quite cozy and sheltered in the little cave created by the drooping branches. The tabby was still sitting where Mandy had left him. He put his head on one side, staring with one wide eye at Mandy.

"It's me again," she said softly. "Don't worry, I won't hurt you."

Very slowly, she reached toward him. The cat didn't move away, and her fingers sank deep into the softest, thickest coat she'd ever felt. The cat blinked his good eye at her and began to purr.

"Mandy?" Her mother's voice called from above.

"I'm in here," she said, easing the big cat onto her lap. "He's a little confused and nervous but I think he trusts me. I'm going to pass him out to you, Mom."

"Hold on to him tightly," Dr. Emily advised. "If he's injured, we don't want him getting frightened and running away."

Mandy wrapped her arms around the tabby and shuffled forward until her mother could reach down and take him from her.

"Look at his eye!" Mandy urged, standing up. She could clearly see the red rim of the tabby's eye, the swollen lid and the telltale moisture.

"Poor thing, it looks like you have a nasty infection," Dr. Emily said.

"What do you think caused it?" Mandy asked.

"I can't be sure until I take a closer look under

the eyelid," Mandy's mom replied. "There could be a little dirt trapped in there and he rubbed it and made it sore. It should be fine after an antiseptic wash." She stroked the tabby's head. "Mandy, is this the cat that belongs —"

"To Wayne Skilton?" Mandy replied, nodding. "Yes. Will you take him to the clinic, Mom?"

"Well, since we know who this gorgeous boy belongs to, I'd feel more comfortable doing that with his owner's permission, sweetheart," Dr. Emily said.

"OK," Mandy said, getting serious. "We'll take the cat to Step-up Cottage and tell Wayne's parents that he needs to be treated right away."

Mandy settled the big cat in her arms. He lay over her forearm like a blanket, with his front paws dangling. He was pretty heavy; James took a turn when Mandy's arm got tired. They walked side by side, hurrying, while the sun slipped lower in the sky and it grew even colder.

"Almost there, boy," Mandy soothed. "Then we'll take you to the clinic and you'll be better in no time." She hoped that the Skiltons were at home. As they approached Step-up Cottage, she warned James: "His name is *Skilton*, remember! Nothing to do with cheese."

"Skilton, Skilton," James chanted under his breath as Mandy knocked on the door.

It opened immediately and a rectangle of bright light spilled out onto the front step. A woman wearing painter's overalls stood in the doorway. She had a wide paintbrush in her hand and was rotating it slowly to prevent it dripping.

"Hello. Can I help you?" she asked, looking from James, then to the cat, and then to Mandy.

"Sorry to disturb you," said Mandy. "Is Wayne here, please?"

"Yes, hang on." She turned and yelled up the stairs. *"Wayne!"*

The tabby cat stiffened in James's arms, arching his back and looking around for an escape route.

Mandy put out a hand and petted him. "It's all right," she said softly. She wondered why Mrs. Skilton hadn't asked about her cat.

There was a loud clumping sound of boots on the wooden stairs. "I can't stop, sorry, or the paint will dry unevenly," the woman said. She hurried off down the hall and through an open door to the right, leaving the front door ajar.

Wayne appeared in the hallway. "Yeah?" he said.

"Hi, Wayne," Mandy began.

The tabby gave a loud meow and began to squirm

in James's arms. "We brought your cat back," James said.

Wayne shook his head. "I don't have a cat." He reached out to the door, as if he was about to close it.

"But he hurt his eye," Mandy blurted out. "We brought him to you because we thought he belonged to you. We want to take him to the clinic."

Wayne shrugged, looking away. "You can take it wherever you want. It's not mine."

Mandy felt annoyed. She knew she hadn't imagined him petting and talking to the tabby the other day, but now he didn't seem to care at all. "Well," she said, trying to keep her temper, "do you know whose cat this is?"

"We don't think he's a stray," James added, "because he's too well cared for — and too friendly."

"Wayne! Why's the door open? All the cold air is coming in," said a tall man who came into the hall from a door at the far end and looked out. "Oh, hello," he said. He looked very surprised to see Mandy, James, and a cat on the doorstep.

"They found a cat," Wayne explained. "They thought it was ours. It needs to see a vet."

Wayne's father cleared his throat. "I'm David Skilton," he said, smiling.

"I'm Mandy Hope," Mandy said. "This is James Hunter."

"That's certainly a great-looking cat you've got there," Mr. Skilton remarked. "But I'm afraid it doesn't belong to us. Wayne can go with you to a few of the neighbors' houses along the road, if you like."

"But I was watching TV!" Wayne started to protest.

His dad held up one hand. "TV can wait. It's time you started meeting some of our new neighbors. And you want to find out who owns this cat, don't you?"

"I guess," Wayne muttered, snatching a jacket that hung on a hook near the front door. He pulled it on and stepped outside.

"See you, Dad," he said, slamming the door behind him.

Mandy took the tabby out of James's arms. She hadn't counted on having to carry him farther than Step-up Cottage. She had been certain he belonged to Wayne, who was sulking so much she wished he had stayed at home.

He walked on ahead of them with his head down and his hands stuffed in his pockets. He paused at the end of a gravel driveway. "There's no point in trying in there," he said, jerking a thumb in the direction of his immediate neighbor's house. "It's pitch-black inside, so they must have gone out."

"OK," James agreed. "What about the next house?"

"I guess we could try there," Wayne said, sounding as if he'd rather be doing anything else.

"Have you ever *seen* this cat before?" Mandy asked him, hitching the tabby higher in her arms. Wayne was acting like he didn't know the cat at all, and Mandy wanted to see if he would admit to having made friends with the tabby before.

"Once or twice," he replied evasively.

The tabby meowed and wriggled to free itself from Mandy's arms. "He doesn't want to be carried anymore," Mandy said. "But I'm afraid he'll run off if I let him go. He really needs to be taken to Animal Ark."

"Animal *what*?" asked Wayne, wrinkling his nose.

"It's the veterinary clinic Mandy's parents own," James explained.

"Cool," said Wayne, and Mandy couldn't tell if he was being sarcastic or not.

They'd reached the front door of the house on the left of Step-up Cottage. Wayne knocked, and after a few moments he cupped his hands around his face and looked in through a lighted window.

"No one's home," he said.

Mandy soothed the cat with her hand. "Let's keep trying," she said.

James and Wayne took turns knocking at the front

doors of promising-looking houses. On each doorstep, Mandy explained why they were there. But even though a couple of people recognized the cat, no one knew who he belonged to.

When they reached the end of the street, Mandy decided they should turn back. The cat was twisting around in her arms, clearly in a lot of discomfort.

"He seems sore," Wayne observed. "Look how he's rubbing his eye!"

The tabby had buried his face in the crook of Mandy's elbow. Only the dark points of his golden ears were visible as he tried to press his eye against her coat sleeve. Suddenly, he lifted his head and looked straight up at Mandy, letting out a mournful yowl that wrenched her heart.

"Poor thing," Wayne muttered.

Mandy was surprised. At last Wayne seemed to be getting worried about the cat.

"Can't *you* do something?" Wayne demanded. He looked at Mandy with a frown. "Aren't your parents vets? Don't you know how to help him?"

"I'll take him to the clinic," Mandy said.

"But he needs help now!" Wayne argued. "I bet he feels much worse after being marched around in the dark like this."

Mandy thought hard. "He might have something stuck

under his eyelid. I've watched Mom and Dad give an
eye bath to cats before, so I could see if that washes
it out."

"OK." Wayne seemed utterly convinced that Mandy
could help. "Come on, then. We'll do it at my house."

They walked quickly through the gathering darkness.
The tabby snuggled under the folds of Mandy's scarf.
She could feel him moving every few seconds to rub his
irritated eye. He was very unhappy, and when he lifted
his face to meow in pitiful protest, Mandy could see
that his eye was still watering. She was desperate to
help him — and soon.

"Hang on," said Wayne, as he was about to open his
front door. "My mom's painting and she won't want us
trooping around. Tell me what you need and I'll bring
it out."

"Just a bowl of warm water and some cotton balls,"
Mandy instructed. "Thanks." In her arms, the tabby
heaved a trembling sigh as if he knew what was
coming.

Wayne quickly came back carrying a plastic mixing
bowl brimming with water.

"Will you hold him, please?" Mandy asked.

Wayne looked surprised. "Me? But I don't know
what to do."

Mandy didn't want to let him know that she and James

had spied on him, even if it had been by accident. "Well, you seem very comfortable around the cat, and I think he'll trust you because he's met you before," she said carefully. She caught James's eye and he nodded.

Looking wary, Wayne gently took the tabby and held him against his chest, wrapping one hand around the cat's front paws so he couldn't struggle. The cat looked from Wayne back to Mandy.

"Poor boy," Wayne said quietly. "Don't be frightened. We won't hurt you."

"James, can you tilt the cat's head back for me?" Mandy asked.

She soaked a cotton ball in the water and squeezed out just enough so that she didn't scare the cat with a deluge. James held the cat's chin with one hand and put his other hand on the back of his neck. Mandy had seen her parents bathing injured eyes dozens of times, and she concentrated on getting it just right — opening the lid wide enough for the water to wash away whatever was making the eye so painful. The cat tensed in Wayne's arms, meowing in protest as she squeezed the water directly into his eye. The cat sneezed and shook his head. A stream of water ran down the cat's cheek and soaked into the sleeve of Wayne's jacket.

Mandy squeezed out the cotton ball and dabbed at the cat's messy cheek. "I think that'll help him," she

announced. It was too dark to see if anything had been washed away in the water but she knew that the tabby's eye would be cleaner and feel soothed by the warm water.

Wayne ran a hand over the tabby's head. The cat seemed bewildered and shook his head again. Then he sprang out of Wayne's arms and onto the ground.

"Oh, no!" said Mandy, trying to grab him. "I still want to take him to the clinic to get a checkup!"

Wayne lunged for the cat as well but it neatly side-stepped him and, with one graceful leap, he was swallowed up by the undergrowth along the fence.

Mandy plunged in after him. Her boots made loud crunching noises as she trampled over the frost-covered plants. "Here, tabby, come on, boy!" she called.

But there was no sign of the cat, not even a tell-tale meow.

"Gone," Wayne said with a note of sadness in his voice.

"It's too dark to go chasing him now," said James, shivering.

Mandy sighed. "There's not much more we can do tonight. Maybe he'll find his way back to where he lives. I hope his owner notices something's wrong and gets real medical help."

Wayne stared at the place in the undergrowth where the tabby had disappeared. Then he turned to Mandy and said, "Come on." He picked up the bowl and tossed out the remaining water. "I'll ask my dad to give you a lift back to your place."

As they pulled up in front of James's house, Mandy saw Blackie with his front paws up on the window ledge, barking a welcome.

"Thanks Mr. Stil . . . Skilton," said James. "See you tomorrow, Mandy."

"Bye, James."

Mandy directed Wayne's father to Animal Ark, thanked him and hurried inside.

"You were gone a while," said Dr. Emily as Mandy came into the kitchen. "What happened with the cat?"

Mandy took off her coat and boots. "It turned out that Wayne Skilton doesn't have a cat!" she said, exasperated. "We don't know who the tabby belongs to."

"But I thought you said —"

"I was wrong," Mandy said. "We knocked on doors up and down Foley Lane, but no one knew where the tabby lived. He seemed so sore and upset that I gave him an eye bath to soothe him. But then he jumped out of Wayne's arms and ran off."

Dr. Emily put an arm around Mandy's shoulders. "Well, an eye bath was definitely the right thing to do."

"But what if it wasn't enough?" Mandy protested. "I should have brought him right back to the clinic."

Dr. Emily gave Mandy another hug. "Try not to worry, dear. We'll just have to hope that the cat finds his way home to his family."

"I hope so," Mandy said. "Oh, Mom, I really hope so."

Five

"You look like you spent the night in a tree," Dr. Adam greeted Mandy as she came slowly into the kitchen.

"I didn't sleep very well," Mandy replied, going over to the cupboard where her calendar hung. "Did Mom tell you? The tabby under the tree *doesn't* belong to Wayne Skilton."

Dr. Adam broke an egg into a saucepan sizzling with melted butter. "I heard and I'm sorry," he said. "He has a home somewhere, though, I'm sure. Mom says he's in good shape except for the eye. Hopefully your eye bath did the trick, and if not, his owners will know to bring him here."

"If he finds his way home," Mandy said, feeling miserable. She pressed the back of the calendar and popped open another of the little doors. Today, she revealed a young male osprey hovering over a stretch of water.

Dr. Emily came in with the newspaper under her arm. "He'll be fine, I'm sure," she said soothingly. "Tea, Adam?"

"Yes, please. Scrambled egg, anyone?"

"I was hoping for another one of your mince pies for breakfast," said Dr. Emily, winking at Mandy.

"They were all eaten!" Dr. Adam said triumphantly.

"Are you thinking of giving up Animal Ark to become a pastry chef, Dad?" Mandy teased.

"Not yet," her father said. "But it doesn't hurt to practice."

Dr. Emily sat down with a mug of tea and opened the newspaper.

"Mom?" Mandy said. "You know the lane where Step-up Cottage is?"

"Yes, Foley Lane," her mother answered. "Why?"

"Well, there's a house at the end of the lane, number eighteen, where the yard's very overgrown. I'd like to ask permission to look for the tabby. Does anyone live there?"

"I can find out," Dr. Emily said. "If they ever had a

pet, we'll have the address in our database, which should give us their name."

"Could you do it now, please?" Mandy asked. "I want to go down there today."

"Sure, I'll go and see what I can find out," said Dr. Emily. "You go get dressed and meet me in the reception area."

"Hey!" said Dr. Adam, as Mandy took the stairs two at a time. "What about breakfast?"

"Catch you later, *chef*!" Mandy called with a grin.

Once she was dressed, she found her mother at the computer, scrolling through the list of patients who lived on Foley Lane. "Mr. Bell has Daisy, and I know she's their only pet. There's Miss Campbell, who keeps ferrets and is allergic to cats. Ah! Mr. Gerald Webb, 18 Foley Lane. He has a cat named Monet."

"That sounds promising," Mandy said.

"Wait a minute." Dr. Emily frowned at the screen. "Monet last visited Animal Ark ten years ago — and he was elderly then!"

Mandy's spirits sank. "Oh," she said. Then she brightened. "Maybe they have another cat?"

"It's worth a try," her mom agreed. "Good luck!"

It was another blustery day. The low-hanging clouds had a hint of yellow in them, and Mandy wondered if it was going to snow. She fastened her padded jacket as she hurried toward James's house, hoping that the tabby cat had somewhere warm to stay. She had wished for snow for Christmas, but now she hoped that any snow would hold off until the tabby could be found. As she passed the tree on the green, its branches laden with colorful lights, she stopped to look underneath, just in case. But the tabby wasn't there.

Outside the Fox and Goose, she saw John Hardy hauling hay bales out of the trunk of his father's station wagon. "Hi, John!" she called. "How are the rabbits?"

John looked worried. "I think Bubbles is getting cold at night," he said. "So I got her some extra bedding. She's sitting really awkwardly, like she has a stiff neck."

"Oh, poor Bubbles! I know what that's like," Mandy said. "I slept in a draft once when I went camping and in the morning I couldn't straighten my head at all. It didn't last for long, though. I'll come and see her a little later. Meanwhile, layer the hay in deep and close up any gaps in the hutch."

"I will," John said. "Thanks, Mandy."

Mandy walked on. She was wondering whether she could put a hot water bottle under Bubbles's bedding at night when she spotted James wrestling with Blackie.

"No," he was saying. "*This* way, Blackie!"

"James!" Mandy called.

Her friend was flushed from his exertion with the Labrador and, as Mandy reached him, she noticed his glasses were steamed up. "He's got a mind of his own today!" James puffed.

Mandy bent down to stroke Blackie. "Come on!" she said in a happy tone of voice. "Let's walk!" She took the leash from James and turned around. Blackie trotted beside her, looking up adoringly with his tongue lolling.

"Where are we going?" James said, hurrying to keep up.

"Foley Lane," Mandy answered.

James frowned. "Again?"

"I want to go back to that old house at the end of the street," Mandy said. "Mom checked and the people who live there once had a cat called Monet. Tabby's probably not Monet, but they were cat owners once, so they might have gotten another one."

They jogged along Foley Lane, partly to stay warm and partly to keep up with Blackie, who was tearing along with his nose to the ground. When they reached the bend in the road, they stopped to get their breath while they looked at the old house.

"It looks pretty empty," James said cautiously.

Mandy shook her head. "There must be someone living there. We saw a light on, remember?"

"OK," James said, tugging at Blackie. "Let's go and knock on the door."

A five-bar gate hung lopsidedly on its hinges. A tangled mass of weeds and plants partly blocked the entrance. Mandy spotted a wooden sign, half hidden by a knot of ivy.

"Gray Wethers," she read, lifting the ivy. "That's an unusual name."

Blackie trotted through the gate, sniffing the ground excitedly. Following him, James held back the branches of a tree and gestured for Mandy to squeeze by. The house was built of gray stone, and its slate roof was patchy with moss. One gutter hung by a nail and creaked in the wind. It stood out, Mandy thought, for being the only house along Foley Lane without a single Christmas decoration.

"You're right. It doesn't look like anyone lives here," she said. "Maybe they moved away and left the light on by mistake."

James went up three wooden steps to a pillared porch. Cobwebs covered the ceiling, and the windows on either side of the front door were grimy. "Wow, look at this!"

The wooden pillars that held up the porch had been carved with intricate scenes of small animals. There were tiny squirrels scampering among ivy leaves, birds on twigs, and acorns clinging to oak leaves.

"Look at this rabbit!" Mandy gasped. "It's beautiful."

"Pretty amazing," James agreed. "Somebody must have loved this house to have gone to so much trouble."

Mandy ran her fingers over the carvings, marveling at each carefully executed detail. "Whoever lives here — or lived here — loves nature and animals," she decided.

"Since we're here, we may as well knock," said James. He rapped on the door with his knuckles. The sound echoed through the house.

Mandy pressed her face to the window. Inside, she could see a hallway and beyond that, through an open door, a room in which there was a piano. A lamp with a red, fringed shade sat on top of it, casting a circular pool of light on its burnished wooden frame. "Look, James. There's a piano and a light on top of it. Who would move away and leave their furniture behind?"

James looked in. When he pulled away he had a smudge of dirt on his nose. "You're right!" he said. He hammered on the door again.

"Hello!" Mandy called. "Anybody home?"

There was no reply.

"I give up," said James. "If only we'd brought a piece of paper and a pen we could've left a note."

"I didn't think of it," Mandy admitted.

Blackie was eager to get on with his walk, and James

almost tripped down the steps trying to keep up with him. Mandy lingered a moment to have another look at the carvings in the wood. "Just amazing," she murmured.

She caught up with James outside the gate. "It seems like a sad place," she said.

"Forgotten," James agreed.

The wind whipped Mandy's hood off her head, and James's nose, under the smear of dirt, was bright red from the cold. They walked briskly and when they reached the bend in the street, Mandy saw someone standing in the Skiltons' garden. "There's Wayne," she said, nudging James.

When he saw them, Wayne waved frantically. "Quick!" he shouted. "I need your help! It's the tabby cat!"

Six

With James and Blackie behind her, Mandy raced along the narrow lane toward Step-up Cottage. She almost crashed into Wayne, who was crouching over the tabby just inside the front gate, his hand under the cat's chin.

"His eye looks worse," Wayne blurted out.

Mandy knelt down to take a look. Her relief that the cat had reappeared quickly changed to dismay. The beautiful tabby let out a small meow when she gently lifted his face but he didn't try to move away. His injured eye was now completely closed, and Mandy saw the signs of infection in the yellowish rim of the cat's badly swollen lid.

"He needs help right away," she said.

"Yikes," James said, arriving breathlessly. "That eye looks nasty."

The tabby kept his good eye fixed on Blackie, who stared back from where James was keeping him at a safe distance.

"See?" Wayne prompted Mandy. "Maybe you shouldn't have put that water in his eye after all."

Guilt flooded through Mandy. What if she had misjudged the situation? She felt like she had let the beautiful tabby cat down, and now he was really sick.

She stood up. "James and I will stay here with the cat. You go and ask your parents if they can take us to Animal Ark. Tell them the tabby needs treatment right away."

"OK," Wayne said. He turned away and headed up the steps to the front door. "And let's get him the *right* treatment this time."

"Uh-oh," said James quietly.

A few moments later, Mrs. Skilton came out of the house carrying a large cardboard box. "Poor cat," she said. "Hello again, you two."

"Hello, Mrs. Skilton," Mandy said. "Thanks for driving us."

"That's all right," said Mrs. Skilton. "I'm sorry you haven't been able to find the cat's owner. Look, I put a folded towel in the bottom of the box."

"That's perfect," Mandy said.

The tabby meowed when Mandy picked him up and lowered him into the box. He sat up and peeped over the edge as she carried him to the car. James held the back door open for her and she got in, holding the box on her lap. Inside, the cat turned in circles, bobbing his head around, and meowing and growling softly. Mandy felt very anxious. She had to wait for James to settle Blackie in the back of the station wagon and for Mrs. Skilton to run back inside to find her car keys. She felt like asking everyone to hurry up! Wayne sat in the front. He looked nervously over his shoulder every time the cat meowed.

"Hold the box steady," Mrs. Skilton advised, as she backed the car out of the driveway. "We don't want the cat jumping out while I'm driving."

Blackie rested his chin on the backseat and occasionally licked James's ear. "Turn left here and then take the first right," Mandy told Mrs. Skilton. The tabby gave a hollow-sounding yowl as Mrs. Skilton braked and the box lurched on Mandy's lap.

"Don't be frightened," she whispered to the cat, holding the cardboard flaps of the box loosely over his head. "We're not going to hurt you."

For Mandy, the short journey seemed to take forever but, at last, Mrs. Skilton pulled into the parking lot of Animal Ark.

"Thanks, Mrs. Skilton," Mandy said.

"Glad to help," she said. "And I'm very glad Wayne has made such nice friends!"

James gave a forced little cough, then thanked Mrs. Skilton. He went around to Mandy's side to take the box from her. Mrs. Skilton got out and opened the back for Blackie, handing his leash to Mandy. Mandy noticed that Wayne didn't look at her as she went past. But she would worry about him later. Right now her only priority was getting help for the tabby cat.

The door to one of the treatment rooms was wide open, and Mandy spotted her mother putting away some veterinary supplies. She wore her white lab coat with a stethoscope around her neck.

"Mom!" Mandy called, looping Blackie's leash over a chair.

Dr. Emily smiled as the three of them, and the cat in the box, squeezed into the treatment room. "Hello. What have you got there?"

"The cat turned up in Wayne's yard," Mandy explained, as James heaved the box onto the table. "But now his eye seems much worse!" She laid a hand on the cat's smooth, golden head. He was nervous, peering around at the strange room with his ears lowered. He raised a paw as if he was going to jump out, but Mandy held him firmly until James had closed the door.

"You must be Wayne," said Dr. Emily, smiling at the boy who was standing in the corner, looking awkward. "I'm Dr. Emily."

"Hi," muttered Wayne, not taking his eyes from the cat.

Mandy's mom pulled on a thin pair of latex gloves and opened the flaps of the box. "Gosh, you really are a beauty!" She allowed the tabby to jump out onto the table. Mandy quickly put one hand on his back and the other on his chest to keep him still.

"So you haven't found out who owns him?" said Dr. Emily, looking at Mandy.

She shook her head. "We knocked on the door of the house on Foley Lane, but no one answered. Maybe they're away and left the light on by accident."

Dr. Emily began by examining the tabby all over. She took his temperature and checked his gums to make sure they were a healthy pink color. Then she listened to his heart and his breathing. The cat coughed when she probed the dense fur around his neck.

"Why are you doing that?" Wayne asked. He had come forward to watch the examination.

"I'm checking to see if his lymph nodes are swollen," she replied. "If he has a flu virus, his glands will be bigger than normal. Some cat flu viruses can cause eye problems."

"Are they swollen?" Mandy asked.

Dr. Emily shook her head. "No, they seem fine."

She reached for a tiny penlight and shone it into the cat's injured eye. Mandy held the tabby's head still. He was very good at first, hardly moving while Dr. Emily felt around the upper and lower lid. Suddenly, he twisted his head away and shook it violently. Mandy's heart leaped in sympathy.

"Sorry, sweetie," said Dr. Emily. "I know you're sore. There must be something stuck in that eye and it's causing a nasty infection." She looked up at Mandy, Wayne, and James. "Even though we don't know who the cat belongs to, I think it's serious enough for me to go ahead and have a good look inside the eye."

The tabby began to meow pitifully as Dr. Emily turned away to fill a syringe. Mandy did her best to comfort him, running one hand softly up and down his spine and encircling him with her other arm to prevent him jumping down off the table.

"What's that for?" Wayne asked as Mandy's mother returned with a syringe. He was looking rather worried.

"We're going to put him to sleep for a while," she explained. "So he won't feel a thing while we have a look in his eye."

There was silence in the room as Dr. Emily shaved away a little patch of the tabby's fur with a small electric clipper, then slipped a needle into his front paw. Within seconds the tabby cat crumpled slowly until he was lying on his side. He breathed steadily, as though he was having a peaceful sleep. Dr. Emily held the injured eye wide open with two fingers and moved her penlight around, looking for signs of damage to the cornea, the part of the eye that gave the cat his sight. Mandy crossed her fingers behind her back; she knew that if the infection was really bad, the tabby could be left blind forever.

"Pass me the forceps, Mandy, please," said Dr. Emily.

Mandy used a sterilized wipe to pick up the instrument from a stainless steel tray and handed it to her mother. Dr. Emily frowned in concentration as she bent low over the cat.

"Ah!" she exclaimed. "There's our culprit! See?"

She focused the beam of light for Mandy, who leaned forward to see. She bumped heads with Wayne and he muttered, "Sorry." In the jaw of the forceps was some tiny thing that Mandy at first couldn't identify. Dr. Emily began to tug at it, carefully working it free, and Mandy saw a shard of a pine needle, about a quarter of an inch long, slide out of the cat's weeping eye! The needle was viciously sharp and would have been agonizing against the cat's tender inner eye.

"Oh, Mom!" she gasped, horrified.

"Ouch!" said James, grimacing.

"It was lodged in the eyelid, rubbing right on the cornea," Dr. Emily explained.

"Is he going to lose his eye?" Wayne asked fearfully.

"No," Dr. Emily said. "I think his troubles are over now. He'll need some antibiotics to get rid of the infection, that's all."

"Oh, thank goodness," Mandy said, letting out a big, relieved breath. "He must have picked it up when he was under the Christmas tree on the green. I wish I'd known . . ." she trailed off.

Dr. Emily slipped an arm around her shoulders and gave her a hug. "You did your best. This lovely cat is going to be fine. Good work, all of you."

The tabby's coat was like burnished copper under the lights. He was stretched out, breathing steadily as if he was having a peaceful sleep. He would make a complete recovery, and Mandy could go on trying to find his owner. She looked up just in time to see Wayne smile. She smiled back. His hand moved gently over the cat's ears, and Mandy saw his face relax. She realized she had underestimated how anxious he had been about the cat.

"I'd better get going or I'll be late for lunch," James said.

Wayne looked up. "See ya," he said, and James nodded.

"Bye, James," said Mandy.

Dr. Emily had stripped off her gloves and was washing her hands at the sink. Mandy stayed by the table, watching the tabby's eyelids twitch as he began to wake up from the sedative.

"Give him a minute or two, and then take him to the residential unit, will you, Mandy?" Dr. Emily asked.

"OK," Mandy replied. When her mom went out, she looked at Wayne. "You should give this cat a name. We can't keep calling him 'Tabby.'"

"Why me?"

"Why not you?" Mandy countered with a smile. "It was your house he came to when he needed help."

Wayne put a hand on the tabby and rubbed his chest. "He's a great cat," he said. "I like his color best of all. It looks good enough to eat, like caramel and fudge." He grinned, looking like a completely different person. "How about Caramel?"

The tabby opened his good eye and rolled over. He stood up shakily, then fell down, but he was on his feet again almost immediately. Gently, Mandy picked him up. She cradled him against her chest and dropped a kiss on his head.

"That's a perfect name. Come on, Caramel, we'll settle you in a nice comfy cage."

Wayne followed Mandy to the residential unit. He slid the bolt on a cage and held the door open while Mandy put Caramel inside. The cat began to carefully explore his cage, padding around and sniffing at the folded blanket. By the time Mandy returned with a bowl of food and some water, he had curled himself up into a tight ball of stripy fur and put his head on his paws.

"We've got to find his owner," said Wayne, looking troubled.

"We will," Mandy said. "Let's let him sleep now. He's had a tiring day."

"I'd better get home," said Wayne, looking at his watch.

"You can come over tomorrow if you want to see Caramel," Mandy offered.

"Yeah, I will," Wayne said. He began to walk toward the door and then he stopped and turned around. "Mandy?"

"Yes?"

"Um . . . thanks," he said. Then he opened the door and was gone.

On Friday that week, school closed early for the Christmas break. Mandy met up with James at the bus stop. He was sitting on his backpack, looking gloomy.

"James!" Mandy chided. "Why do you look so miserable? It's almost Christmas!"

"Oh, I'm happy about school closing," James told her, standing up as the bus rumbled into view. "It's just that I've got to go to the dentist this afternoon. I hate the dentist." He hauled his backpack up the stairs of the bus and took a seat next to Mandy. "How's Caramel?"

"Restless," she replied. "He wants to get out of that cage. I don't blame him. He's feeling so much better."

"We could have gone looking for his owner this afternoon if it wasn't for . . ."

"I know," Mandy said sympathetically. "The dentist. We can look for his owner tomorrow instead. OK?"

"OK," James said.

Mandy got up. "I'm getting off here," she told James. "I'm going to the pet store to buy John's rabbits a treat!" She jumped off the bus and turned to wave at James, whose nose was pressed to the window. He waved back, still looking glum.

In the shop, Mandy was tempted to buy Blackie a rawhide chew that looked like reindeer antlers, or a bright red-and-green-striped collar, but she decided to spend her allowance on the bunnies instead. Now that Caramel was so much better, she could spend more

time with John's rabbits. She hoped that in the three days since she'd seen her, Bubbles was back in high spirits. She chose a packet of dried alfalfa chews and a packet of pellets she knew to be a bunny favorite.

"They're very healthy, too," the assistant assured her.

Back at home, she raided the fridge for fresh vegetables and found a crisp green head of broccoli. With all of the treats in a plastic bag, she set out for the Fox and Goose. She headed straight for the yard when she got there. There was a biting, blustery wind blowing, and none of the rabbits were in their outside run. The shed door was closed, too. Mandy headed inside to look for John. She found him in the living room, kneeling on the floor, surrounded by shiny wrapping paper.

"Hi," said Mandy, surveying the chaos from the door.

"Come in," John said. He was wielding a pair of scissors, slicing through the brightly colored paper. There was a piece of Scotch Tape in his hair.

Mandy smiled. "You look busy."

"I'm making some surprises for the rabbits," John told her. Among the shredded wrap, Mandy saw seven small canvas stockings in a neat row, each stuffed with toys and treats for the rabbits.

"Oh, they'll love those! What a great idea!"

John turned red. "They're just little things," he said,

sounding shy. "Rabbits love to forage, so they'll have a good time trying to get the stuff out of the stockings."

"I brought a special treat for Bubbles," Mandy said. "But it's not for Christmas. It's for now. Can I take it out to her?"

"Yeah, she's in the shed," he said.

"Are you coming?" Mandy asked, carefully stepping over the mess on the floor.

"I'll be down in a minute," John answered.

Mandy made her way through the back of the restaurant, waving to Mrs. Hardy in the kitchen as she passed. Outside, daylight was fading. Mandy shivered and zipped up her jacket as she headed for the shed. She opened the door and looked in. There was the scurrying sound of paws on the floors of the hutches. She flicked on the light and crouched down beside the first hutch. Barney had his nose pressed to the wire, twitching a cautious greeting. He thumped his hind foot to warn the others of Mandy's presence.

"It's only me." Mandy chuckled. She stood up and walked along to the hutch that Bubbles shared with her mother. "Bubbles? Where are you, little girl? Are you feeling better?" Crouching down, Mandy peered into the hutch. Button was stretched out with her eyes almost closed. There was a thin stalk of hay sticking out of her mouth.

"Hi, Button. Where's Bubbles?" Mandy said, surprised that the bunny hadn't hopped up to the mesh to say hello. She peered to the very back of the hutch — and gasped.

Bubbles's head was turned awkwardly. One eye looked at the ceiling of the hutch, the other at the straw under her feet. At the sound of Mandy's voice, she tried to straighten her head, but she couldn't.

"Oh, Bubbles!" Mandy cried. "What happened to you?"

Seven

Mandy scrambled away from the hutch and stumbled out of the shed, startling the other rabbits. She heard them darting away, scurrying into their sleeping compartments.

"John!" she shouted, racing across the yard.

She collided with John as he was coming through the back door. He was eating an apple, and Mandy sent it flying.

"Oh!" John said, surprised, as his apple rolled away into an empty flower bed. "What's the matter?"

Mandy took a deep breath. She might scare John if he knew how anxious she was about Bubbles. Yet she could only think that the little bunny had something seriously wrong — why else would her head be twisted at such an impossible angle?

"Nothing," she said. "I mean, there is . . . something wrong, I mean."

John looked quizzically at her. "Is it Bubbles?"

"Yes." Mandy nodded miserably. "She's in her hutch and her head is turned completely sideways. I don't think she can move it. She's . . . much worse, John. But don't worry, because —"

John began to run. "Get your parents, will you?" he shouted over his shoulder.

"OK," Mandy called. Putting her head around the door of the kitchen, she had to raise her voice to get the attention of an assistant chef. She was using a food processor and making a terribly loud noise.

When she finally looked up and switched off the machine, Mandy asked, "Is Mrs. Hardy here?"

"Not now, dear," the assistant chef replied. "She went out with Mr. Hardy."

"Can I use the phone, please?" Mandy asked.

"In the front hall," she said. "Help yourself."

Mandy dialed Animal Ark, hoping one of her parents would be available. If not, she and John would have to crate the little rabbit and carry her over to the clinic, which could make Bubbles even more stressed. She was very relieved when her father answered. She quickly told him about Bubbles.

"Do you know when John first noticed that something was wrong?" he asked, sounding calm and practical.

Mandy felt a pang of guilt. "It's not a new problem," she admitted. "She hasn't been well for a few days. John said he thought Bubbles was acting like she had a stiff neck, but I just saw her and it's much worse than that! She can't move her head the right way around at all! Could you come over and see her?"

"I'll be right there," Dr. Adam promised.

"Thanks, Dad." Mandy hung up. She felt dreadful. Why hadn't she had the sense to realize that Bubbles had needed veterinary attention when she first showed signs of being sick? Why hadn't she advised John to have the rabbit checked out instead of agreeing that extra bedding would solve her problem?

As bad as she felt, Mandy realized that feeling sorry for herself was not going to help her friend. John would be very worried. He needed Mandy's support and reassurance right now. She raced back outside to the shed. John had opened the door to Button and Bubbles's hutch wide, and Button was crouched in the doorway to the sleeping compartment, watching with beady bright eyes. But Bubbles hadn't moved.

John sat cross-legged on the floor beside the hutch

and was reaching in and stroking the bunny softly. "Is someone coming to see her?" he asked Mandy as soon as she appeared.

"My dad's on his way," she said. "He won't be long."

Mandy didn't think she'd ever seen an animal look as sick as Bubbles. The bunny's cheeks were wet, as though she had been crying. She was tucked up into herself, quivering as if she were exhausted with the effort of trying to turn her head. Mandy tried to be

calm, both for the sake of the rabbit and for John, but awful images kept popping into her head. What if Bubbles had a tumor that had been growing in her spinal cord and would eventually paralyze her? Or what if she had somehow broken her neck, and the fracture had worsened until there was nothing anyone could do?

The minutes ticked by slowly, and at last Dr. Adam arrived. As soon as she heard the sound of his boots on the gravel, Mandy dashed outside to meet him.

"I'm so glad you're here, Dad. I'm so worried. And John's a mess. I don't want him to know how bad it could be, but what if it's a tumor?

"I know you're nervous," Dr. Adam said, shifting his black bag to the other hand to link an arm through Mandy's as she tugged him along to the shed. "But a tumor is the worst possible case. There are other causes for this sort of symptom that we need to rule out first. Let's just have a look at her, OK?"

But Mandy saw a look of deep concern on her father's face when he crouched down in front of the hutch and saw Bubbles. She sat down beside John; her legs were trembling and she didn't think they would hold her up much longer.

Dr. Adam greeted John as he set down his big black bag on the ground. "Sorry to hear about Bubbles, John," he said. He reached into the hutch. "Let's have a look at you, honey bunny."

John shifted back and hugged his knees while he watched Dr. Adam lift Bubbles out. Mandy's dad sank his fingers into the soft fur around the rabbit's neck, checking for swollen glands, then asked Mandy to hold Bubbles still while he took her temperature. He examined her abdomen, pressing gently with his fingers. He looked at her teeth and her eyes, which was tricky with her head twisted so severely. Bubbles made small squeaking sounds of protest, and her legs pummeled the ground as she tried to escape.

"OK," Dr. Adam said at last. He put Bubbles back into the hutch. "I'd like to do a more complete examination," he said, putting a hand on John's shoulder. "I'm pretty sure she has a condition known as torticollis, or head tilt, which is usually caused by an ear infection. But I need to rule out any other possibilities. Whatever case, she's going to need treatment."

"Is she going to be OK?" John asked, sounding fearful.

"I'll do my best to make sure she is," Dr. Adam promised. Mandy gulped — that wasn't the same as saying yes.

"Her temperature's a bit low and she's probably dehydrated and hungry on top of everything else," Dr. Adam went on. "It's difficult to drink or eat when your head isn't where it should be." He stood up and brushed the dirt off the knees of his trousers. He gave Mandy's shoulder a squeeze. "Come on," he said. "Let's get her into the carrier I have in the Land Rover and drive her over to the clinic. The sooner we start her treatment, the better chance she'll have to recover."

Back at Animal Ark, Mandy held Bubbles on an examining table for her father. The rabbit's long, velvety ears drooped and she shuffled in Mandy's grip, her nose twitching and her breathing quick and shallow. She was clearly very distressed.

"Torticollis is not a single disease," Dr. Adam explained. "It's a symptom of a problem with the rabbit's balance system. It usually means the middle or inner ear is infected, though in more serious cases, it can be a problem with the central nervous system. So I'm going to have a look inside her ears," he said, reaching for an instrument with a long nose.

"Ouch," said John, as he watched Dr. Adam push the tube gently into Bubbles's ear. The rabbit twitched under Mandy's hands, trying to straighten her neck, and Mandy held her tighter.

"Not much longer, little one," she promised under her breath.

"Aha!" her father said, peering into his end of the instrument. "It's infected, that's for sure. I'm going to take a sample and send it away for a culture test."

John made a face. "Poor Bubbles, having fluid in her ear!"

"Yes, that's why she's been so unbalanced," said Dr. Adam. "It's pressed on a delicate system of bones in the ear known as the vestibular apparatus, which has made her very dizzy and unable to hold her head the right way up."

"What are you going to do to help her hold her head straight?" John asked.

"I'm going to give her antibiotics to kill the bacteria that causes the fluid," he said. "Once the infection goes away, her head will go back to normal."

"Is it painful?" asked John, rubbing Bubbles's nose with a finger. The bunny seemed exhausted from trying to wriggle free from Mandy's grasp, and now she flopped onto the table, panting hard with her back legs outstretched.

"More uncomfortable than painful," Dr. Adam answered. "You'll have to hand feed her and hold her water bottle for her until her neck relaxes, OK?"

"No problem," said John, sounding relieved and determined at the same time. But he still frowned while Bubbles was injected.

"I want to bring her temperature up now," Mandy's dad said. "We need to make sure she stays nice and warm."

"Should I get a heating pad?" Mandy offered.

"No," said Dr. Adam, shaking his head. "A rabbit's skin burns very easily. But you could fill an old sock with uncooked rice, tie a knot in the top, and put it in the microwave for a couple of minutes. It'll heat up much more gently than an electrical pad and will stay warm, too. Bubbles can cuddle up to that instead."

"OK," said Mandy, and sped off through the connecting door to her home to dig out one of her socks. When she returned, she found John in the residential unit, holding Bubbles in his arms.

"You can put her in there," Mandy told him, pointing to one of the smaller cages. John gently lowered Bubbles inside. She hopped to the far end and lay down in a corner. She blinked, her head still wrenched at an awkward angle.

"It's so hard to watch her," said John, sounding tearful. "It looks horrible."

"I know," said Mandy sympathetically. "Let's make her more comfortable. I'll get some old towels. Dad says that rabbits with head tilt sometimes roll around, and we don't want her to hurt herself against the sides of the cage."

When they had built up a barrier of padding, Mandy filled a clean water bottle and John held it while Bubbles drank. He seemed to cheer up as he watched her draw the water eagerly. Bubbles refused the dried pellets Mandy offered, so she left the bowl in the cage. Their final task was to fill the sock with rice and warm it in the microwave. John helped Mandy tie a good, tight knot in the top. Mandy tucked it under one of the towels, and the little rabbit lay down and rested her soft brown cheek on it.

"She's going to be fine," Mandy said, smiling at John. "The medicine will start to work soon, and she's safe and warm."

"I'll come and see her tomorrow," John said. "Thanks, Mandy."

"That's all right," Mandy said. "Don't worry. I'm sure she'll be home in no time."

When John left, Mandy visited Caramel. He was asleep, stretched out comfortably with one chocolate-colored paw covering his nose. Mandy spent a minute admiring his luxurious coat. It shone with good health. He couldn't have been gone long from his home with a coat in such great condition! It was a mystery.

Caramel woke up. He opened his good eye and yawned. Mandy smiled at the sight of his perfect pink tongue and snowy teeth.

"Hello, gorgeous," she said.

The cat got up and rubbed his forehead against the door of the kennel, purring. Mandy put her fingers through the wire and scratched his head. His infected eye looked less red and the swelling had gone down, but it was still closed. She opened the cage door to give him a really good scratch on his head.

"Hello," said a voice behind her.

Mandy turned to see Wayne standing in the doorway. The feisty little dachshund a few cages down began to yap a welcome. "Hi, Wayne," Mandy said. "Come and see how well Caramel's doing."

Wayne came over and put his hand out to the cat. Mandy saw him smile as Caramel pushed his muzzle into Wayne's palm. "I brought him a piece of fish," he said. "Do you think that's all right?"

"He'll love it!" Mandy said.

Wayne fumbled with the plastic wrap he'd brought and held out the chopped-up fish to the tabby, who wolfed it straight from Wayne's hand.

"Leftovers from dinner," Wayne said, adding, "My dad's outside in the car. He said he'd drive me around to see if I can find Caramel's owners. Do you want to come?"

"Yes!" Mandy said. "That'd be great. I'll get my coat. Can we pick up James on the way? I know he'll want to come with us."

"Sure," Wayne said. "I'll wait here with Caramel while you get your coat." He turned back to the cage, and Mandy heard the beautiful tabby let out a rumbling purr as Wayne stroked his ears. She suddenly wondered if it was worth going out to look for Caramel's owners after all — what if the perfect owner was right in front of her?

Mr. Skilton waited in his car while Mandy tried to persuade James to part with his grilled cheese sandwich and leave immediately to search for Caramel's owner.

"But I haven't eaten all day," James protested. "I had a filling at the dentist and I was all swollen. . . ."

"Bring the sandwich with you," Mandy suggested. "But hurry up! Mr. Skilton is waiting!"

"OK," said James, suddenly cheerful. He folded the grilled cheese sandwich in half and took another bite. "I'm ready."

"Hi, James," Mr. Skilton said, as James got in the back of the car.

"Hello," mumbled James, his mouth full.

"Now, where to first?" Mr. Skilton asked, turning to look at Mandy.

"Let's go back to Foley Lane," she said. "We still have some houses to try along there."

"No problem," he said, and started the car.

It was only a five-minute journey, and soon Wayne's father slowed to a stop at a house on the corner of the main road and Foley Lane. "Let's ask this woman," he suggested. "I spoke to her once before about garbage pickup and she seemed very friendly."

Mandy saw a tall woman in an overcoat and rubber boots descending the steps to her driveway. Mandy remembered seeing her in the post office, though she didn't know her name. The woman looked ready to go out. Car keys dangled from her gloved hand.

"I'll go," Mandy offered, getting out of the car. "Excuse me!" she called. "Can you help us, please?"

The woman glanced around, looking puzzled, but her face relaxed into a smile. "Of course," she said. "Are you lost?"

"No." Mandy shook her head. "We live in Welford. My parents run Animal Ark."

"Ah, yes." She smiled. "How can I help?"

"We found a tabby cat and we're looking for its owners. Do you know of anybody we could ask?"

"I *have* seen a tabby cat around," said the woman thoughtfully. "Is it a large cat?"

Mandy nodded, her heart leaping with hope. The woman went on: "Unusual coloring? Sort of stripy gold?"

"That's exactly right!" Mandy said.

"Yes, I remember thinking that it was beautiful. I'm pretty sure it lives down at the end of the street. Go right to the end of Foley Lane until you can't go any farther. There's an old house down there," she said. "I've seen the cat coming out of the driveway a couple of times."

"Oh!" Mandy said. "Is that Gray Wethers?"

"That's right," the woman confirmed. "I can't be certain, but I'm pretty sure the lady who lives there is the person you need to speak to."

Mandy shook her head. "We knocked on the door but there didn't seem to be anyone living there."

"Oh? Well, I'm pretty sure Mrs. Webb hasn't moved away. Perhaps she was in the yard. Why not try again?" she suggested.

"Okay, we will." Mandy smiled. "Thank you." She hurried back to the car. Her hopes were high.

"Bull's-eye!" Mr. Skilton declared, when Mandy relayed the message. "Gray Wethers it is, then."

"But we've been there twice already," James said. "It's deserted."

"Are you sure?" Wayne said.

"Mr. Webb still lives there," Mandy said confidently. "The one who owned Monet, remember? That's what the woman said. Let's go and try again, anyway."

"I'm only the chauffeur," said Mr. Skilton, looking at Mandy in the rearview mirror. "What are my orders?"

"To Gray Wethers," said Wayne and Mandy together.

They soon pulled up at the broken-down gate that led to the old house. Mr. Skilton stayed in the car, listening to a football game on the radio, while James, Mandy, and Wayne got out.

"I'll be right here," he said. "Call if you need me."

"You're right, James," Wayne said, peering down the driveway. "It looks like nobody has taken care of this place for years."

But Mandy was picking her way determinedly through the tangled foliage and fallen branches to the front door. She shivered. The wind made the old house creak and threatened to snatch her woolly hat from her head. She gave a sigh of thanks that Caramel and Bubbles were tucked in safely at Animal Ark under the expert care of her parents.

"Out of my way," James growled, flicking a climbing rose that tried to snag his sleeve.

Mandy waited for Wayne and James to reach the porch before she knocked on the door. She saw James stumble as a gust of wind whistled through the branches, ruffling the pages of a yellowed newspaper. A single page flew up and flapped for a second against his chest. Then the wind plucked at it, and it went whirling away.

"What's this?" James said. Carefully, he removed a small curl of paper that had become stuck to his sleeve. "FINNIGAN'S FINEST TUNA FOR CATS!" he read.

"It must be the label from a can of cat food," said Wayne, looking excited. "The people who live here must have a cat, right?"

"What people?" said James, climbing the steps to join the others. "I don't see any signs of actual people."

"Everything all right?" Mr. Skilton called from the car.

Wayne turned and gave his father the thumbs-up sign, then turned back to Mandy. "Knock," he urged. "Go on."

She raised her hand and knocked on the door.

In the moment's silence that followed, there came a faint sound from behind the door. Mandy put her ear to the crack. "I can hear a piano!" she whispered.

As she listened, the music stopped and a radio announcer began to talk. Mandy knocked again, louder.

"You see?" James said when nobody answered. "No one lives here. They must have left the radio playing to make people think there's someone inside."

"James!" Mandy hissed. "Look!"

Through the small pane of frosted glass above the knocker, a looming, wavering shape had appeared. It grew steadily larger.

"Someone's coming!" Mandy said.

Eight

The heavy wooden door gave a groan of protest and slowly opened.

A very frail elderly woman peeked around the edge. Her head was level with Mandy's shoulder, and her face was pale and lined with soft creases. The hair around her face was a wispy cloud of white, caught at the back in a neat little bun. Her blue eyes were bright, and she wore a brooch studded with purple stones where the collar of her shirt was buttoned at her neck. On her feet were a magnificent pair of slippers embroidered in scarlet and gold and green.

"Please," she said politely, "I'm not buying anything."

She began to close the door, but Mandy sprang forward.

"Wait!" she pleaded. "We've come about a cat."

Seconds passed before the door opened slowly again. The old woman looked out, an expression of confusion on her face. "*My* cat? A golden tabby?" she said, her voice faint. "Have you found him?"

"Yes," Mandy said. "We found him under the Christmas tree on the village green. His eye was infected because a piece of pine needle was stuck in it."

"Oh!" she said, sighing. "I've been so worried. How is he? Where is he now?"

"He's much better," Mandy replied with a smile. "We took him to my parents' veterinary clinic, Animal Ark."

"That was very kind of you. Thank you!" she said.

"These are my friends," Mandy said. "Wayne and James. We would have told you sooner, but we didn't know who Caramel's owners were."

"Caramel?" Mrs. Webb echoed, sounding puzzled.

"It's the name we gave him," Wayne explained.

"Ah, I see." She nodded. "Very sensible. Well, his real name is Vermeer. When can he come home?"

"I'll have to check with my mother," Mandy told her. "But it'll be in the next day or two, I'm sure."

"That's wonderful news!" chirped Mrs. Webb. "I've missed him very much. And it's terribly good of you to have taken the trouble to help him. Of course, I'll need to make arrangements to have him picked up. I don't drive, you see."

Mandy smiled at her. "I'm sure my mom or dad could bring him back for you."

"He's a lovely cat," James piped up. "Very friendly."

"Yes, he's been a great companion to me."

Mrs. Webb was so soft-spoken and dignified; Mandy liked her a lot. But she looked very thin, and there was something about the way she stood clutching the edge of the door that made Mandy think she might not be too steady on her feet — and it was *very* cold. No wonder she hadn't been out looking for Vermeer.

"I look forward to having him home again," said Mrs. Webb, smiling her thanks again. She began to close the door.

"Excuse me?" Wayne said. "Um, can I ask about these carvings?"

Mrs. Webb looked around the door again. "Ah!" she said. "You noticed! They're wonderful, aren't they?"

"Yes," Wayne said. "They're great."

"My husband, Gerald, was a furniture maker," Mrs. Webb continued softly. "Carving was his passion. He made some of the pews in Welford Church. Of course, that was years ago." She stopped and a rosy flush came to her face.

Mandy ran her fingers over the carvings, marveling at how much patience Mr. Webb must have had to create so many tiny, but exact, details. She wished she could wash away the accumulated grime on the pillars, perhaps even polish the wood so it gleamed as it must have done once upon a time.

"Well," Mrs. Webb said, "I mustn't take up any more of your time. Thank you, all of you, for helping Vermeer." She turned to Mandy. "You'll give him a kiss for me, won't you?"

"Yes," Mandy said. "I will. Good-bye, Mrs. Webb."

Mandy, Wayne, and James grinned and high-fived each other as they went down the steps to Mr. Skilton's car.

"We did it!" Mandy announced happily, climbing in. "We found Caramel's owner!"

"Yes," James added, fastening his seat belt. "The right house at last."

"She was a nice old lady," Wayne said. "The cat's real name is Vermeer, Dad."

"Good for you!" Mr. Skilton said, turning off the radio. "Would you like to come over for a hot drink?" he asked Mandy and James. "You'd be very welcome."

Mandy glanced at Wayne but she couldn't tell if he wanted them to stay for a while or not. "Um, OK, thanks," she said, looking at James, who nodded. "We'll stay for a little while, thanks."

"She must be lonely," Wayne said, as his father switched off the engine outside Step-up Cottage. "Mrs. Webb, I mean." He got out of the car, and Mandy followed him to the front door. He led them through the hall and into the kitchen.

"Any luck?" asked Mrs. Skilton. She plucked off a pair of yellow rubber gloves and let the water drain out of the sink.

"Yeah," Wayne replied. "The cat lives down at the end of the street, at number eighteen. He belongs to an old lady named Mrs. Webb."

"Good news," Mrs. Skilton said, pouring milk into a saucepan to heat. "And good work, you three! If she's an older lady, it's understandable that she couldn't get out to look for her cat. Does she have anyone living with her?"

"I don't think so," Mandy said.

"What about her husband?" James asked. He took a mug of hot chocolate from Mrs. Skilton and blew on it. "The man who carved the animals on the wooden pillars?"

"We don't know if he's still alive," Mandy pointed out. "She spoke of him in the past tense."

She looked at Wayne. He didn't look very cheerful.

"Mrs. Webb doesn't need to be lonely here," she said. "Welford is a lovely, friendly place to live. Everyone is so nice, really."

Wayne looked up and caught her eye. Then he looked away quickly.

"I'd better go," James said. "Blackie will be wondering where I've gone." He got up and carried his mug to the sink. "Thanks for the hot chocolate, Mrs. Skilton."

Mandy stood up, too. "Thanks for having us over," she said. Then she turned to Wayne. "You can still come and visit Vermeer while he's in the residential unit if you want."

"Can I come tomorrow?" Wayne asked, brightening.

"OK," Mandy said.

That night, Mandy woke up tangled in her sheets after a particularly vivid dream. All of the tiny, hand-painted animals on her Advent calendar had come to life and marched around her bedroom — everything from barn owls to ferrets and mice — demanding food and a warm place to sleep. Bubbles was there, too, and so was Vermeer, wearing a black patch on one eye like a pirate.

She turned over and snuggled down under her comforter, trying to fall back to sleep. But early morning light was seeping around the edges of her curtains, so it was impossible. There were too many exciting things going on right now — treating Bubbles; finding Caramel's, no, *Vermeer's*, owner; getting ready for Christmas. She got up and tiptoed downstairs in her robe. She went straight to her calendar and pressed opened the door. This time she revealed a beautiful little painting of a fawn, its head bent over the waters of a tumbling stream. Mandy smiled and hung it back on the door handle.

She filled the kettle for her parents and thought about hunting around for one of her father's delicious mince pies, but just then he appeared in the doorway, yawning.

"You're up early," he said.

"I had a strange dream," Mandy told him. "How about you?"

"I've got a lot of paperwork to catch up on," Dr. Adam said. "I thought I'd get an early start."

"If you're going into the clinic, can I come and say hello to Vermeer and Bubbles?"

"Sure," said Dr. Adam. "Let's make some tea and take it with us. Mom's sleeping in."

Mandy went upstairs to change, taking care not to wake her mother. In the residential unit, she discovered that Vermeer had recovered his voice. As soon as Mandy stepped through the door, he rubbed his head against the front of his cage and meowed a loud welcome. When Mandy didn't move across the room quickly enough, he turned around and pawed at the small pile of towels she had laid out for him, gnawing at the cotton and kneading it with his feet, like a kitten.

"How is he?" asked Dr. Adam, coming in behind her.

"He definitely seems better," Mandy said.

She unbolted the door of the cage and reached in to give Vermeer a stroke. He stared intently at her, his one golden eye round and bright. His injured eye was only half closed now, and the swelling had almost entirely gone down, although it still looked rather watery. He stretched out his front leg, and Mandy felt it tremble as he braced his paw against the palm of her hand. The pad of his foot was warm and soft and pink. Vermeer purred loudly as he pressed his hard, translucent claws against her hand, but he didn't hurt her a bit.

"We found your owner," she told him, as he lifted his head and affectionately butted the underside of her chin. "Mrs. Webb," Mandy said the name aloud as if he might recognize it. "Soon you'll be going home to her."

She stood aside as her father leaned in to check Vermeer's eye. He nodded approvingly, then straightened up and handed Mandy a tube of ointment from a cabinet above their heads.

"Would you please put some of that around his eye?" he asked. "I've got to get started on my paperwork or I won't be finished before the clinic opens."

"OK, Dad," Mandy replied happily. There was nothing she liked better than being useful in the clinic.

"Wash your hands well first," he reminded her.

But Mandy had already closed Vermeer's cage door and was heading for the bathroom.

She washed her hands thoroughly and then went back to Vermeer's cage. At the sight of her, he began to purr, a lovely, rumbling sound that seemed to come from deep inside. He lifted his head up to greet her, and she put her left arm over his back and held on to his chest, using her index finger to push up his chin. With her right hand, she deftly squeezed the ointment into the corner of his injured eye. Vermeer jumped back and shook his head. He sneezed and glared at Mandy, obviously annoyed.

"Sorry." Mandy smiled, petting him. "It's over now, and it's going to make you better."

Vermeer blinked at her, his eye glistening with the ointment. Mandy brought him a fresh bowl of water and his morning meal and then left the residential unit to raid the fridge in the staff kitchen. She came back and headed straight for Bubbles's cage.

The rabbit could smell the apple Mandy held in her

hand. She shuffled to the front of the cage, her little nose twitching. Her head was still tilted at an odd angle, so that the tip of one long ear brushed her bedding, but Mandy felt very hopeful that she'd be interested in her fruit snack.

"Hi, Bubbles," she said. She unbolted the door and offered Bubbles a slice of apple. "How are you feeling today?"

Bubbles sniffed the apple all over, but then turned away. Her head drooped so that her ear was almost flat on the ground. Mandy ran her fingers gently through her soft, warm fur. "You must try and eat something," she told her. "You won't get better unless you do."

"How's she doing?" asked Dr. Adam, popping his head through the door.

Mandy sighed. "She doesn't look any better. Her head is still twisted around and she won't eat, either. I'm really worried about her."

Mandy's dad pushed open the door and came in, carrying a mug of fresh tea. "It's hard to look at her and *not* worry, isn't it?" he said. "Deep-seated ear infections take a long time to clear up. And the truth is, sweetie, we don't yet know if she's going to make a full recovery. There could be permanent damage to the inner ear, if the infection has been nasty enough."

"What does that mean?" Mandy asked as she watched

Bubbles shuffle away to a corner of the cage and rest her head awkwardly on the folded towel.

"Well," Dr. Adam said, placing his hand on Mandy's shoulder, "hopefully the antibiotics will clear the infection, and Bubbles will be right as rain in a few days."

"But if they don't?" Mandy prompted.

"If they don't," he went on, "then her balance and her hearing might be permanently affected. That's because the tiny nerves in the inner ear can be damaged so badly they no longer send the correct information to the brain to tell the rabbit which is the right way up."

Mandy bit her lip. Bubbles could end up deaf and paralyzed! She wondered if she should tell John to call Bubbles's owner. But she decided to let it go for another day or two in the hope that the little rabbit would recover.

Dr. Adam went on. "If she doesn't start to drink or eat soon, I'll give her subcutaneous fluids through a drip. That will balance out the electrolytes in her system and keep her properly hydrated."

"OK," Mandy said. "I think I'll go and see John. He'll want to know how Bubbles is. I'm not going to tell him everything, though."

"Why not?" her father asked.

"He's worried enough already," Mandy said. "If I tell him there's a chance Bubbles could be deaf and paralyzed, he might give up hope that she'll ever get better."

Dr. Adam nodded. "OK. And keep your spirits up," he added. "She's getting the very best care here."

"I know," Mandy said, leaning into the cage and kissing Bubbles on the side of her head. "I'll be positive. But I don't think John's going to enjoy Christmas unless Bubbles is completely well."

There had been a sprinkling of fresh snow during the night. Crossing the village green on her way to the Fox and Goose, Mandy thought the Christmas tree looked magical under its strings of colored lights and natural decorations. Her breath clouded around her like smoke as she walked across the backyard of the Fox and Goose.

John wasn't in the shed. When Mandy pulled open the door, she saw the rabbits tucked up in their hutches in a deep and warm litter of hay, paper fiber, and processed wood. She longed to hug each one of them in turn, but she didn't want to disturb them. They looked so peaceful, dozing with their paws tucked under them and their eyes lightly shut.

A grating noise led her to John. He was in back of the shed, sawing at a piece of wood balanced across two tree stumps. His nose was bright red, and he wore

not one but two thick woolen hats. He was concentrating hard on his task, which, Mandy guessed, had something to do with the rabbits' obstacle course.

"John!" Mandy had to shout before he heard her.

He looked up and groaned, pressing his palm to the side of his head. His face was flushed and his eyes looked very bright. "Sorry, I didn't hear you. I don't feel very well. I think I'm getting a cold."

"Oh, what a time to get sick!" Mandy said sympathetically. "Is there anything I can do to help?"

John gave a rueful grin. "No, thanks. I just want to make a start on my obstacle course for the rabbits. Otherwise, it'll be time to go back to school and it won't be finished." He put down his saw. "How's Bubbles?"

"Um, she's doing all right," Mandy said carefully. "My dad's keeping a close eye on her. . . ."

"But she's definitely getting better?" John insisted.

"She's more comfortable now," said Mandy, adding, "I hope *you* feel better soon."

John didn't reply. Instead he said, "I'd like to come and see Bubbles today. Is that OK?"

"Of course," Mandy said, smiling. "Come anytime."

Mandy shook the snow off her boots at the back door of Animal Ark. She pushed open the door, savoring the smell of buttery toast.

"There you are!" said Dr. Emily. "You were up early this morning! You've got a visitor."

Mandy turned around from kicking off her boots. Wayne stood by the sink, looking a little awkward.

"Hello!" Mandy smiled. "Did you come to see Vermeer?"

"Yeah," Wayne said. "How is he?"

"He seems much better," Mandy replied. "And even friendlier than usual! I just put some ointment in his eye."

"Can we take him to Mrs. Webb?" Wayne asked.

"Not today," Mandy answered. "My dad wants him to stay here while he's on the antibiotics."

"Okay," Wayne said. He held out a bulky package. "Oh, um, I wanted to show you this."

Mandy's mom placed a teapot on the table. "Would anyone like some toast? Mandy? Wayne?"

"Yes, please, Mom," Mandy said. She took the package from Wayne. It was wrapped in layers of plain paper. She laid it on the kitchen table and slowly peeled off the paper to reveal a single piece of wood carved in the shape of a kestrel. The head of the falcon was perfect, with bright eyes and its beak open, and its wings were spread in flight.

"Wow," she said. "This is *amazing*. Thank you so much! Where did you get it?"

"It's not for you," Wayne said, going bright red. "Sorry, I mean . . . it's mine. I made it. I thought I might take it to show Mrs. Webb. Her husband —"

"Was a wood carver!" Mandy finished. "What a great idea. It's so realistic, even the eyes . . . and the beak! You're really good, Wayne."

"Do you think she'd like to see it?" Wayne asked. "You don't think she'll get sad, thinking about her husband?"

"I think she'd *love* to see it," Mandy said, remembering how delighted Mrs. Webb had been when they admired the carvings on the porch. "Let's have some toast. James will be here in a little while, and then we can go and surprise Mrs. Webb together!"

Nine

James soon arrived with Blackie, who was leaping around at the end of his leash in unusually high spirits. He was so eager for some exercise that Mandy suggested they walk to Gray Wethers.

"It's cold," Wayne pointed out.

"We'll warm up if we're walking," James said. "Mandy and I are used to long hikes."

"And a walk would make Blackie very happy," Mandy added.

Wayne shrugged. "All right," he said.

Mandy called good-bye to her mom, who was upstairs. Their breath condensed around them in the cold air as they crunched down the driveway. Wayne pulled up his hood so that only a tuft of fair hair peeped out. The wooden sign for the clinic swung in the wind, creaking on its hinges. The fields, spreading up toward the Beacon and High Cross Farm, were frosted with white. It reminded Mandy of her Advent calendar, and she almost had to check that there weren't any little doors with numbers on them in the fields.

James started a conversation about school; he was obviously making an effort to make Wayne feel comfortable. Wayne replied in monosyllables at first, but soon he was telling them how he planned to try out for the soccer team, and what he thought about their science teacher, Mr. Pym. He was in the same year as Mandy at Walton School, but in a different class. By the time they reached Foley Lane, Wayne's hood had fallen back; he kept up easily with James, and his cheeks were flushed a rosy pink from the cold. Mandy thought how much easier he was to get along with now. Maybe he had stopped wishing he was back in Manchester.

"Here we are!" James announced when they arrived at the gateway to Gray Wethers. He looped Blackie's leash around a sagging fence post and told him to sit and wait. Stepping up to the front door, he knocked three times.

After a few moments, Mrs. Webb opened the door, just a crack, and peered out. "Hello!" she said, opening the door wider. "Have you brought my darling home? How is he?"

Mandy smiled. "He's much better, Mrs. Webb, but my dad would like him to finish the course of antibiotics before he comes home. But," she added, "he's doing really well!"

"Well, thank you so much for coming to tell me how he is." Mrs. Webb started to close the door.

"Mrs. Webb?" Wayne said quickly. "Um, I wanted to show you something." He held out the wrapped carving. Mandy stepped away from the door to give him room.

"Oh?" Mrs. Webb's frail hand held tightly to the door frame.

Wayne pulled the kestrel from its covering. It lay in his outstretched palm as if the burnished brown bird had just landed there. Mrs. Webb reached out to take it and ran her fingers lightly over the polished wood.

"Did you make this?" she asked.

"Yes, I did."

"Oh, how Gerald would have loved to see it! My husband, you know . . ." She trailed off. "It's really very, very good. Gerald would have thought so, too."

"Did you really make that?" James whispered, nudging Wayne.

Wayne nodded. He looked pleased. "I'd like to see the pews your husband carved, Mrs. Webb," he said. "I'm very interested in wood carving, you see."

Mrs. Webb hesitated, her bright eyes roving over the gathering at the door. "Yes. You'll have to go into the church, of course. Gerald was very proud of those pews! Wonderful wood, too." She smiled. "But his favorite way to make his carvings was to collect old bits of wood and interesting sticks he found. He could make the tiniest twig come to life as a bird or an animal." She weighed Wayne's carving in her hand, then suddenly opened the door wide.

"Come in," she said. "It's been a long time since I had any visitors, so you'll have to excuse the mess. I'd like to show you something."

She led the way into a small sitting room, walking slowly across a wood-plank floor that was smooth and polished and didn't have any rugs on it. In spite of her warning, it was very tidy, and Mandy noticed that there was no television. Bookshelves lined two sides of the room, their books stacked perfectly in order of height. Mrs. Webb eased herself into a red brocade armchair that seemed to engulf her. She put out a hand to switch off a little portable radio that was playing softly on a small table beside the chair.

"There, do you see?" Mandy looked to where she pointed. "On the table under the window? Those are some of Gerald's carvings. Go over and have a look."

Mandy, James, and Wayne stood in a row, gazing down at the tabletop. There were more than twenty figures of birds and animals; some big, some small, others tiny. They had been made from a variety of different colored woods, carved by expert, nimble fingers into lifelike replicas.

"These are fantastic!" Mandy said. "Can we touch them?"

"Oh, yes," Mrs. Webb replied. "Do pick them up."

"Wow, look at this!" James exclaimed, choosing a carving of a fox. Mandy saw two fierce-looking canine teeth in the creature's open mouth.

"I like this roe deer," said Wayne, tracing its hooves with his fingers.

The carvings ranged in size from minute brown-backed beetles to a family of badgers, each twice as big as Mandy's hand. They were so beautifully made that Mandy felt as if they might start tumbling playfully together at any moment.

"Mr. Webb must have loved animals," Mandy said.

"You're right, dear," said Mrs. Webb. "Gerald and I spent a great deal of time enjoying nature — and learning from it, too. Animals and birds are so much more sensible than us, don't you think? They don't have silly quarrels or wars."

Mandy admired a beady-eyed oystercatcher with a wedge-shaped beak and long, skinny legs; then she stroked the glossy back of a rabbit standing on its hind legs. The curious expression on its face reminded her of Bubbles.

"I'll never be this good," Wayne said, picking up one of Gerald Webb's carvings of an osprey, head cocked and wings outstretched.

"You will," Mrs. Webb told him. "With practice, and if you really like it, I'm sure you will be as good. You've made a start with the kestrel."

"Which is your favorite, Mrs. Webb?" asked James, who was examining a carving of a plump and contented-looking cat. "I like this cat best, I think."

"That's Monet," Mrs. Webb said. "A cat we had for fifteen years. He's very special to me. Gerald has captured his likeness perfectly. He always was a bit too fond of his food. But he was an excellent mouser, so it seemed only fair to let him eat what he caught. But let me see. . . . Perhaps my absolute favorite is the field mouse. My husband made it for me when we got married."

Mandy soon spotted the tiny, dozing field mouse. It

had been made from a walnut shell, smoothed into the sleeping form and curled into a tiny ball with its tail wrapped around it like a blanket. "It's adorable!" she said.

Mrs. Webb nodded. "A cute little thing, isn't it?"

Mandy looked at the pictures on the wall. Hanging above the fireplace was a large oil painting of a mist-shrouded field. The hills were smoother and flatter than the Yorkshire moors that she knew so well, so she knew it was not a local picture. Two circles of standing stones were in the foreground, and Mandy's curiosity drew her closer. On a small brass plate at the base of the frame she saw the words GRAY WETHERS.

"Gray Wethers," Mandy read aloud. "That's the name of this house!"

"Those are ancient standing stones on Dartmoor in the southwest of England," Mrs. Webb explained. "I met my husband there, so naturally we took it as the name of our home."

"How romantic!" Mandy said, smiling.

The walls between the tall windows overlooking the yard were covered with a series of small watercolor paintings that showed different wildlife scenes, from open fields with rabbits and sheep to woodlands full of squirrels and shy deer. They seemed oddly familiar to

Mandy. Could she have seen them in an art gallery or on Christmas cards? She had definitely seen the picture of the fawn drinking at the stream very recently. And she knew the squirrel with his cheeks bulging with food, too. . . .

Of course! They were from her Advent calendar!

"What a coincidence!" she exclaimed. "You've got some paintings by Matilda Richards! I got an Advent calendar painted by her from my grandparents this year.

I love her pictures." She glanced at Mrs. Webb, wondering why the old lady hadn't said anything.

Mrs. Webb was looking down at her hands, neatly folded on her lap. Her cheeks had turned rather pink. "Well, guess what? I'm Matilda Richards," Mrs. Webb said quietly. "That was my name before I married."

Mandy stared at her in amazement. "Wow!" she said. "Well, thank you . . . uh . . . I mean, I love my Advent calendar . . ." she trailed off, not knowing quite what to say.

"I'm glad," said the old lady, smiling. "I thought that sort of thing had gone out of fashion years ago."

"No way." Mandy shook her head. "I'll bring it to show you, if you want. Even though the pictures inside the doors are tiny, they look exactly like real animals. You'll be impressed with how well they've been scaled down to fit."

Mrs. Webb rested her head against the back of her chair. "That's kind of you, dear," she said. "But there's no need. You see, I'm not able to see my pictures anymore."

There was a moment's silence. James and Wayne had been studying the carvings, but both of them turned curious heads and looked over at Mrs. Webb. Mandy looked around the living room, noticing again how neat and tidy everything was. She suddenly understood why there were no rugs on the bare floorboards, or a television — and not even a newspaper or a magazine was visible.

"Are you — ?" Mandy began.

"Blind?" said Mrs. Webb. "Not completely. I can tell that there are three of you, for example, and I can find my way around the house. But I can't read anymore or see Gerald's beautiful carvings. My eyesight has been failing for quite some time. It's the reason I stopped painting."

"I'm sorry," Mandy said, feeling very sad. Everything she knew about Mrs. Webb fell neatly into place. Of course she hadn't been able to go out searching for Vermeer! Naturally, she was suspicious of people coming to the front door. It must be so hard to meet people and make friends — even in a village like Welford.

"We could do some shopping for you, if you want," she offered. "Or help with things that need doing?"

"Ah, now, that's kind, but there's no need for that," Mrs. Webb said briskly. She didn't seem comfortable talking about her loss of sight. "My son brings me what I need every two weeks, and I manage very nicely, thank you. Now, I really must get to making my lunch. Have you seen enough of the carvings?"

"Yes, thank you," Mandy said, stepping away from the table. "I'll bring Vermeer to you when he's ready."

Reluctantly, Wayne replaced a carving he had been inspecting and gathered up his kestrel. "I think they're great," he said. "Thanks for showing us."

They said good-bye to Mrs. Webb, who waved at them from her chair as they headed for the front door. "Close it tightly on the way out, please," she called. "And you'll bring Vermeer as soon as you can, won't you?"

"Yes, I promise," Mandy said.

"Thanks again!" Wayne called just before he shut the front door behind them. He gave it a little push to make sure it had closed properly.

Blackie barked a welcome, jumping up and wagging his tail. As James petted him for his patience and untied the leash, he looked at Mandy. "Blind! That's really sad," he said.

Mandy bit her lip. "I hope I didn't offend her by offering to help."

"I don't think she wants any help," Wayne said unexpectedly. "I mean, not in a practical way. My grandma in Manchester is just like that, even though she can't walk very well. She doesn't want to think that she's losing her independence, or to be treated like a batty old woman. What she wants are friends!"

No wonder Vermeer is so important to Mrs. Webb, Mandy thought, feeling very pleased that she'd been able to help the injured tabby. "I'm so glad we met her," she said, and James and Wayne nodded.

They left Wayne at Step-up Cottage and headed back toward Animal Ark. Even Blackie was lagging when Mandy and James reached the clinic. His tongue was lolling and he lay down on the flagstone floor in the kitchen with a sigh. James went to get him a bowl of water.

Mandy's grandmother was in the pantry. She was standing on a stool peering at the top shelf.

"Hi, Gran!" Mandy called, and the stool wobbled.

"Oh, you startled me!" said Dorothy Hope.

"Have you lost something?" Mandy asked, steadying the stool with both hands.

"No, I'm trying to find the recipe your father used to make those magnificent mince pies!" she answered. "He just *won't* tell me what he put into them to make them so special."

"Great chefs never reveal the secrets of their recipes," James announced, putting down a full water bowl for Blackie.

Dorothy Hope stepped down from the stool and shook her head in frustration. "Well, I can't find the recipe in here, that's for sure. I'll just have to keep pestering him until he gives in."

"Guess who we met today," Mandy said, flopping onto a chair.

"Who?" her grandmother asked absently. She was flipping through the pages of a cookbook.

"Matilda Richards!" Mandy said triumphantly. "You know, the artist who did the paintings in my Advent calendar!"

"Really?" Dorothy Hope looked up, impressed. "Where?"

Mandy sat down and told her grandmother all about Mrs. Webb, Vermeer, the wood carvings, and how she'd recognized the watercolors on the wall of her sitting room.

"She's blind," James put in. "And she seems quite lonely."

"Lonely?" said Dorothy Hope. "In Welford? How can she be?"

"Well," Mandy explained, "we don't think she gets out very much. She lives at the very end of Foley Lane, and her son only visits every two weeks. Her husband died a long time ago, I think."

"But she's very proud," James put in. "She doesn't want people to start feeling sorry for her."

Mandy's grandmother thought for a moment. "I

wonder if she might like to give a talk at the Women's Club?" she said. "We're always on the lookout for interesting people to give talks, especially people who are local artists."

Mandy shook her head. "I don't think she's very eager to go out — not in the wintertime, anyway," she said.

"Well, I'll go and visit her," said Mandy's grandmother. "I can't believe she's been in the village all this time and I've never met her. I thought I knew everybody here!"

"She's very nice," James said. "You'll like her, and Vermeer is the friendliest cat I've met in a long time."

"Vermeer? That's the name of a great Dutch painter," Gran said. "Great name for a cat, too!"

"Mrs. Webb's other cat was called Monet," said Mandy. "We learned about him at school when we studied French Impressionist painters. That makes sense, I guess, for an artist to name her cats after other artists!" She stood up. "I think I'll go and ask Mom or Dad exactly when Vermeer can go home. Coming, James?"

"Blackie's worn out," James said. "I think I'll take him home."

As Mandy headed into the clinic, she wondered how she could involve Mrs. Webb in Welford village life without looking as if she felt sorry for her. It's true her house was immaculately tidy and she seemed very happy to live alone, but there must be some things that she needed help with. What if Vermeer took himself for a walk around the village again and she couldn't find him? Mandy wrinkled her nose, worried. She needed to come up with a plan!

Ten

Vermeer was fast asleep, nestled into his blankets. His big paws trembled and twitched in a dream; Mandy wondered if he was hunting through the overgrown flower beds in Mrs. Webb's garden, or stalking a bird in the branches of a tree. In the cage beside him, Bubbles was resting with her bedding bunched under one cheek. Mandy's heart sank when she saw how sad the little rabbit seemed. Bubbles looked at her but she showed no interest in moving. Her food bowl seemed untouched and the fresh broccoli lay undisturbed where Mandy had left it.

"This must be Vermeer," said Mandy's grandmother, bending forward to look at the big tabby. "He's got such a wonderful, thick coat. Look at the size of those paws!"

Mandy turned away from Bubbles. "Yes, he's very special," she agreed. "Golden tabbies are rare, too, because they are descended from a single line of cats."

Vermeer woke up, yawned, stretched, and then delicately rubbed his sore eye. He padded over to the stainless steel bars of the cage and put out one white paw. Mandy took it in her hand and squeezed it. The cat meowed and pulled it back. Mandy thought she could hear the frustration in that meow. He was longing to get out of the cage.

"He wants to come out," Gran observed. She slid open the bolt on the door and reached in to scratch the tabby under his chin. "Hello, you gorgeous thing!"

"That gorgeous cat is fine today!"

Mandy and her grandmother turned to see that Dr. Adam had come into the unit. He tugged affectionately on Mandy's ponytail and tucked his stethoscope into his top pocket. Then he had a closer look at Vermeer, holding the cat under his chin and tilting his face so he could look closely at his eye. "Much better," he announced. "No oozing at all."

"Dad," Mandy said, barring the tabby from leaping free of his cage, "can Vermeer go home today?"

"He is better, sweetie, but he will need medication over the next ten days," Dr. Adam said as he slid the bolt closed on the cage door. Vermeer sat down, looking defeated. "He needs to have antibiotic drops in his eye twice a day, as well as the ointment."

"Oh, dear, that might be a problem for Mrs. Webb," Gran said. "Mandy tells me that the cat's owner is blind."

"She can't paint anymore," Mandy said. "Isn't that sad? Mrs. Webb is the same person as Matilda Richards, Dad, the artist who painted my Advent calendar."

"Really?" Dr. Adam looked interested "You're right. It's very sad that she's lost her sight, and I can imagine how much she must be missing Vermeer. But I'm afraid his medication might be too much for her to cope with."

"I can help!" Mandy cried. "I can ride over every day on my bike and put the drops in for her. I could put his food down and keep an eye on him. . . ."

"I can help, too, if it comes to that," said her grandmother, sounding determined.

"And James will, too," Mandy went on.

Dr. Adam laughed and held up both hands in surrender. "OK! If you are all prepared to be on call for Vermeer, then he can go home. But give me one more night so I can be absolutely sure that eye isn't going to produce any more signs of infection. Then, if all is well, he can go home in the morning."

Mandy stood on tiptoe and planted a kiss on her father's bearded cheek. "Great!" she said. Then she turned back to the cage. "A few more hours, Vermeer, and you'll be out of here! Just in time for Christmas."

The rest of the day seemed to crawl by. Mandy couldn't wait for the next day to come so she could see the reunion between Mrs. Webb and her beloved cat. She passed the time helping her grandmother clean the kitchen cabinets, a task her mother tried to achieve each year in the month before Christmas. But this year, Dr. Emily had been too busy even to make a start, so Mandy and her grandmother were doing it for her.

"When Vermeer goes home," Mandy said, stacking items from the pantry on a counter, "poor little Bubbles will be all alone in the residential unit. What a lonely Christmas for a baby bunny — and it'll be sad for John, too."

"Yes, I'm sure John misses her," Gran said. "I hope Bubbles begins to perk up soon."

Mandy tried to imagine the rabbit as she had been not long ago — racing around in the run at the Fox and

Goose. She was smiling to herself, wiping down the shelves at the same time, when her mother came in.

"Oh! You *angels*!" Dr. Emily exclaimed. "Where would I be without you?"

"Eating out-of-date food?" Mandy joked, holding up a can of cherries with an October expiration date.

"Oh, dear!" Gran chuckled from behind a cardboard box she had dragged from the depths of a large cupboard near the sink. She groaned playfully as she stood up and heaved it onto the kitchen table. "What on earth is in here, Emily?" she asked. She opened the cardboard flaps and peered inside.

"I have no idea," Dr. Emily said, filling the kettle.

Mandy's grandmother let out a cry. "Well I *never*!"

Mandy and her mother looked at her. Her cheeks had gone bright pink with indignation. She brandished a shallow box that she had hauled out from the bigger box, stamped all over with the red-and-green lettering of a well-known bakery. LUXURY MINCE PIES, it read.

"Baked those mince pies himself, did he? Secret ingredients to a special recipe? I don't think so! Oh, Adam Hope, you've taken the whole village for a really good ride!"

Mandy and her mom collapsed with laughter. "He

must have bought every box of luxury mince pies the bakery had to offer!" said Dr. Emily.

"What a sneaky trick to play!" said Gran.

"Well," Mandy said, wiping tears from her eyes. "Let's look on the bright side. At least Dad won't be abandoning Animal Ark to become a chef any time soon!"

After supper, Mandy was sitting by the fire untangling a string of Christmas lights when there was a knock at the back door. She jumped up and ran into the kitchen to open it. A blast of icy air blew in. John Hardy stood under the light. He looked very pale and there were charcoal circles under his eyes.

"What's up?" Mandy said, ushering him inside. "You don't look good."

"You know, I've been feeling funny for a few days . . . sort of dizzy," John said, unwinding a long woolen scarf from around the lower half of his face.

Mandy led him through to the living room and made him sit down next to the fire.

"I just saw the doctor and he says I've got an ear infection that's affecting my balance. He's given me some antibiotics and I've got to keep warm," he finished, looking miserable.

"Just like Bubbles!" said Mandy, feeling very sorry for him, though it was an extraordinary coincidence that he had come down with the same infection as the rabbit. It wouldn't be the same virus, but it was still a stroke of bad luck for both of them. "Oh, poor you."

"Yes, I'm even more sorry for her now that I know how she's feeling," he said. "Can I see her?"

"Bubbles? Of course!" Mandy said. "Come on. I'll take you."

In the residential unit, Mandy switched on the light and took John over to Bubbles's cage. The little brown rabbit was sitting with her face to the door and her eyes open wide. Her head was still at an awkward angle, but there was an alertness about her that Mandy hadn't seen for a long time.

John crouched down next to the cage. "Hello, girl," he said.

As Mandy opened the door, the bolt slid back with a twanging sound, and the bunny jumped visibly. Mandy felt like whooping for joy. "She definitely heard that!" she said. Perhaps her hearing would be OK after all.

Bubbles shuffled toward the open door of the cage and put her face into John's outstretched palm in a typical gesture of bunny affection. A thin stalk of broccoli trailed from her mouth.

"I think she's got her appetite back," Mandy said, pointing to the food bowl. "She's eaten something since I last checked on her. Her neck seems a little bit more relaxed as well. The medication must have started to work!"

John smoothed Bubbles's ears. "I *really* hope so," he said.

"It won't be long before she's home with you, exploring your obstacle course," Mandy said confidently.

John smiled. "Do you think so?"

Mandy nodded.

"It would be the best Christmas present ever!" John said. As he spoke, Bubbles went over to investigate a rubber ring lying in the far corner of her cage. She picked it up and hopped back to John with the toy in her mouth.

"Oh, Bubbles!" Mandy said. "You really are feeling better!"

"OK," John said, smiling. "I'm glad I've seen her. I feel better about her now. But I'd better get home. I told Sara I'd only be a few minutes." He sneezed, stepping away from the cage just in time. "Thanks, Mandy."

"That's OK, John," she said. "I hope you feel better soon, and don't worry about your bunny — she's definitely on the mend!"

When she opened her calendar the following morning, Mandy was delighted to find a tiny painting of a field mouse, curled into a snug little ball under a mound of soft snow.

"It's Mrs. Webb's field mouse!" she said out loud. It was identical to the one her husband had carved for her out of a walnut on the day of their marriage.

She pulled on her boots and her jacket and hurried into the residential unit to get Vermeer. He was sitting up in his cage, looking out. When she saw Mandy, he pressed himself against the cage door, reaching an impatient paw through the bars, first one paw, then the other.

"I came to take you home!" Mandy cried, sliding open the bolt. She lifted him into her arms and kissed his cheek. His magnificent tail swished as she went in search of her mother; her palm supported his chest and his front legs hung down on either side of her forearm.

Dr. Emily was pulling on a long, warm coat at the door that led into the clinic. She was carrying a cardboard box. Mandy's dad was on the telephone.

"What's that you've got, Emily?" asked Dr. Adam, when he'd hung up.

Mandy's mom chuckled. "The last of your secret stash of *store-bought* mince pies," she said. "They're for Mrs. Webb." She put a hand out to Vermeer. "Hello, there."

Dr. Adam looked sheepish. "I've been found out then."

Mandy grinned. "Honestly, Dad! You didn't think you were going to get away with pretending to be an incredible baker, did you?"

"It was worth a try." Dr. Adam scratched Vermeer at the base of his tail. The tabby half closed his eyes and purred. "Take care of yourself, young man," Dr. Adam told him.

"Don't you want to put him in a carrier for the journey, love?" Dr. Emily asked.

Mandy shook her head. "He's too well behaved to worry about that." The cat gave a low, rumbling purr as if in agreement.

Mandy's mom plucked her car keys from a hook in the reception room. Mandy soothed Vermeer by running a hand down his spine as she carried him to the car and eased onto the backseat with the tabby on her lap. Vermeer looked around with interest, sniffing the air. Then he lay down on Mandy's lap and amused himself by dabbing his paw at the buttons on her jacket.

When they reached Gray Wethers, the cat slithered out of Mandy's grasp the moment she opened the car door. She saw him loping toward the house and she hurried after him, striding up the three stone steps to the front door. She was certain that Vermeer knew exactly where he was, but Mandy didn't want to miss one moment of his reunion with Mrs. Webb! The tabby rubbed his cheek on the welcome mat and kneaded it with his big paws, purring loudly.

"He certainly knows he's home," said Dr. Emily as she joined Mandy on the top step.

"Look how happy he is to be here!" Mandy said, reaching up to knock on the door.

As soon as the door began to open, Vermeer squeezed through the gap like quicksilver. There was a gasp of delight, then the door opened all the way to reveal Mrs. Webb beaming down at her beautiful tabby cat.

"Vermeer!" she exclaimed. "You've come home!"

Mandy felt a lump swell in the back of her throat as she stood on the doorstep, watching the delighted expression on Mrs. Webb's face. The tabby wound himself around her legs, butting her knees with his forehead.

"My lovely boy," she murmured, picking him up. The cat looked huge against her tiny frame. He rubbed his chin against her ear, making her smile. His front paws hung over her shoulder as if he was hugging her back. Mandy could hardly see for the tears filling her eyes as she watched Mrs. Webb bury her face in Vermeer's coat.

"How I missed you!" she whispered. Then she looked up, her cheeks pink. "Please come in . . . I'm so sorry. Hello, Mandy, dear."

"Mrs. Webb, this is my mom, Dr. Emily Hope," Mandy said, swallowing hard.

"How nice to meet you. Thank you both," said Mrs. Webb, who had still not let go of her cat. Vermeer turned his head and blinked at Mandy, flexing his paws in contentment.

"I'm so glad we could bring Vermeer back where he

belongs," said Dr. Emily. "He's much better, but he still needs medication. Eyedrops and ointment twice daily for ten days."

Mrs. Webb frowned.

"I'll help you," Mandy offered quickly. "I can ride my bike over and —"

"I'll help, too," said a voice from farther inside the house. "I'm closer."

Who's that? Mandy wondered, looking past Mrs. Webb. Wayne Skilton was standing in the doorway of the living room!

"Come in, please," Mrs. Webb said, bending to lower her big tabby to the floor. "I've got the fire on. Do excuse the mess, Dr. Hope."

She led the way into the living room with Vermeer trotting beside her like a dog. Wayne stepped back behind the dining table. Mandy stopped dead in the doorway and gasped. It looked like he had upended the contents of a trash can all over Mrs. Webb's table! Pieces of clay, pinecones, sprigs of holly, rolls of twine, a stapler gun, and several felt-tip pens littered the polished surface.

"Hi," said Wayne, turning red. "We're making decorations for the walnut tree outside."

Mrs. Webb beamed. "Wayne and I have decided the

outside of my house needs a little brightening up, in honor of the season. Isn't he doing a fine job?"

Mandy was still getting over her surprise at finding Wayne hanging out with Mrs. Webb. She found her voice. "Yes, he is. They're lovely!" At one end of the table lay a neat row of varnished twigs and an almost perfect ball of holly; pinecones and acorns were sprayed gold and stuck together in festive-looking bunches.

"You're both doing an excellent job," Dr. Emily agreed, fingering a tiny, silver-sprayed pinecone.

"Gerald and I used to make all of our decorations," Mrs. Webb explained. Mandy smiled when she saw that Vermeer was sitting on one of her shoes. "My eyes might not be as good now, but I can still use my hands." She invited Mandy and her mom to sit. Dr. Emily showed Wayne how to administer Vermeer's drops. Watching Wayne's concentration as her mother explained, Mandy realized that Wayne was completely relaxed in Mrs. Webb's gentle company. He'd found a friend — just as she had found a friend in him.

". . . so I'll come by next week and check up on him, but he's really well on the way to full recovery," Dr. Emily finished.

"Thank you, dear," Mrs. Webb replied. She settled back in her big chair, and Vermeer jumped into her lap. He stood up on his hind legs and rubbed his nose gently against her chin.

"Can I help you decorate the walnut tree?" Mandy asked Wayne.

"Sure. We've probably got enough decorations now."

"Thank you, Mandy," said Mrs. Webb. "Off you go, before my neighbors think I've forgotten about Christmas altogether!"

Wayne loaded the decorations in a shallow cardboard box and shrugged on his coat. Mandy followed him out of the front door. The tree, stripped of leaves and quivering in a brisk breeze, stood at the front of the house, next to the steps. Mandy delved into the box and pulled out a sprayed pinecone on a string. She hung that first, followed by the wreaths of prickly holly and the acorns, which glinted in the pale sunshine and twirled merrily on bits of twine. Wayne had climbed into the lower branches of the tree to tie a bunch of gold pinecones to a higher branch.

"That looks great!" said Mandy. She stepped back a few paces to admire their handiwork.

There was a rap on the window. Mandy looked up to see her mother and Mrs. Webb watching them. Dr. Emily appeared to be describing the tree.

"She likes it," Wayne said, waving to the pair at the window. "She's smiling."

Mrs. Webb *was* smiling. Mandy watched Wayne fix the holly ball to the uppermost branch of the walnut tree, then jump down.

"It looks gorgeous!" she said.

"Yeah," he said. "It's different, that's for sure."

"The most unusual tree I've ever seen," Mandy agreed. "And that makes it special!"

On Christmas Eve morning, Mandy had a pang of conscience. As she opened the last little window of her calendar — a red fox with a magnificent plumy tail — she began to worry about Mrs. Webb spending Christmas Day alone.

"Poor Mrs. Webb," she said, looking at her mom. "Christmas is a time for family and friends."

Dr. Emily looked up from the gift she was wrapping. "I wonder if she'd like to join us here."

"I'd like to ask her," Mandy said. "Can we go and visit her?"

"I'm going over to Foley Lane a little later to check on Mr. Anderson's sheep," Dr. Emily said. "We could stop by if you like."

"Yes please, Mom. I want to make sure she's OK — and we can say hello to Vermeer!"

Mandy spent most of the morning with Bubbles. She had permission to take the little rabbit outside, and she was thrilled to see the bunny investigate the wintry flower beds with curious little sniffs. Her neck wasn't entirely back to normal, but Mandy thought it looked far less alarming; the angle gave Bubbles a quizzical air, as though she had cocked her head to one side in order to listen more carefully.

It was a busy Christmas Eve in the clinic, and Dr. Emily was delayed by a visit from Jack Spiller and his daughter, Jenny, who brought in their old sheepdog. The dog had ripped a claw, which needed stitches. Jean Knox, the receptionist, was helping.

"I've still got some shopping to do!" she told Mandy in an urgent voice, and Mandy kindly took over for her, cleaning up the surgery.

When all was done and the waiting room was empty, Mandy hurried back to the living room to wrap up some Christmas presents. She had just tied a bow on her grandmother's gift when she heard the flap of the letter box open and shut with a *ping*. When she popped her head out of the door, she could see a tiny parcel lying on the hall floor.

FOR BUBBLES, FROM SANTA, read the card attached with a red-and-green ribbon. Mandy grinned. "John's such a good Santa, he even delivers gifts to the bunnies who aren't at home for Christmas! Now I can play Santa, too!"

By the time her mother was ready to leave, Mandy had finished all her wrapping and completed the cards she had made herself. She stuffed them under her bed, grabbed a jacket, and joined her mom in the parking lot. The air was crisp and bright and very cold. They drove to Foley Lane with the Land Rover's heater on full blast.

"We should ask Ernie Bell to have a look at patching this place up a bit," Dr. Emily suggested as she pulled up outside the rickety gate. "Maybe your father would give him a hand. . . ."

"Good idea," Mandy said.

She got out of the car and immediately recognized the distinctive meow coming from under the tree. Vermeer popped out from under Mrs. Webb's walnut tree, calling out a loud welcome to the visitors.

A strip of gold ribbon was draped over one of his ears.

"Oh, Vermeer!" Mandy laughed. "Look at you!" She picked him up and cuddled him. He put a gentle paw on her cheek as she carried him to the front door.

"I keep finding you under trees," she told him. "And I couldn't think of a better Christmas gift!"

Mrs. Webb was very pleased to see them. She had

been sitting by the fire in her easy chair, listening to an audio book. "It's a thriller," she explained. "I just got to the scary part, so I'm glad you came when you did."

Mandy was relieved to see her looking so happy. Perhaps the old lady's life was not as bleak as she had imagined.

"Mandy, your grandmother stopped by to see me," said Mrs. Webb. "It was lovely to chat with her. She's going to borrow a few of my watercolors to display in the village hall with other local artists. I feel very honored."

"Oh, what good news!" Dr. Emily said.

"Fantastic!" Mandy agreed.

"Actually, we came to invite you to join us for Christmas dinner," Dr. Emily explained.

Mrs. Webb didn't reply right away, so Mandy rushed on, "You are welcome to bring Vermeer, if you want to. I'm sure you don't want him to be alone here."

"That's a very kind invitation," said Mrs. Webb. "*Very* kind. However, I've already accepted an invitation to join Wayne's family . . . and they, too, have asked me to bring Vermeer. There's going to be a portion of turkey especially for him!"

"Oh, good!" Mandy said, meaning it. It seemed as if everyone had made new friends this Christmas.

Impulsively, she leaned down and gave Mrs. Webb a hug.

The elderly lady squeezed Mandy's hand. "You're a dear," she said softly.

At that moment, Vermeer padded over and nudged Mandy's knee. She picked him up and buried her face in the velvety fur between his ears.

"Do you know," Mrs. Webb began, smiling up at Mandy and Mrs. Hope, "I *did* think it was going to be rather a bleak Christmas this year. But all that changed when you discovered my lovely tabby under the tree. Now, not only do I have my Vermeer back in good health but some wonderful new friends as well!"

Mandy looked into Vermeer's golden eyes and smiled. "You've got a touch of Christmas magic about you, don't you, boy?" She kissed him on the top of his head and lowered him to the ground.

"Yes," Mrs. Webb continued, "I think that, after all, it's going to be a very merry Christmas." She looked down at her tabby, who had jumped onto a chair and curled into a chocolate-and-gold-striped ball of lustrous fur.

"I think so, too," Mandy said. Vermeer was back where he belonged, Bubbles was recovering, and Mrs. Webb had been welcomed back into Welford's busy social life. It was going to be a *great* Christmas!

Ben M. Baglio's

Where animals come first

Look for Animal Ark®
CORGI IN THE CUPCAKES

Glancing back at the house, Mandy thought how excited Carole was going to be to hear she'd be catering for a very important person. It was a good thing Gran didn't get a chance to give away her identity. If Edward knew it was the Carole he used to date, he might have changed his mind about the order.

Suddenly, Mandy realized that Edward was about to find out exactly who Carole was. "He'll see her name and phone number on the box!" she gasped. "And he'll put two and two together. Then he won't order the cupcakes after all."

"Of course he will," said Gran, slowing down to drive around a branch the wind must have just blown down. "Carole and Edward must have gotten over their relationship a long time ago. And Edward's not the kind of person who'd refuse to buy something just because of a teen romance."

"He'd be crazy if he did," said James. "Those cupcakes are way too good!"

"I guess you're right, Gran," Mandy said. Now that she'd met Edward, she couldn't imagine him refusing to do business with someone as nice as Carole. And knowing how polite he was, it was a mystery why he'd ignored her letters all those years ago.

The stallion statue loomed up ahead. Mandy was thinking again how real it looked when something very real flashed across the path, missing the van by inches. She barely had enough time to make out what it was before it dove into a tree behind the statue and vanished.

"Did you see that huge bird?" she exclaimed.

"I saw *something*," said James. "I thought it was another branch falling down."

"It was definitely a bird," Mandy said. "And it looked like it was falling, the way it hurtled into the tree."

"It was probably just a pigeon," said Gran. "They do fly rather recklessly."

Mandy looked back, craning her neck as she tried to glimpse it again. "Maybe," she said uncertainly. "But I thought it looked a lot bigger than a pigeon."

It was lunchtime when they finished the deliveries, so Gran dropped Mandy and James at Animal Ark before going on to Carole's. "Oh, Carole said to let you have one of the boxes of leftover cupcakes," said Gran. "To thank you for your help."

"Awesome!" said James, who dashed around to the back.

He opened the door, and Mandy reached in to get the cupcakes. There were a few boxes at the back, on the bottom rack. On the shelf above them, a plastic water bottle was lying on its side, leaking. She could see a gash in it, where the water dripped out. It plopped onto the cake box below. "Oh, no," Mandy said, hoping the cakes weren't ruined. But as she leaned in and pulled the box toward her, she uncovered something soft, furry, and the color of toffee, lying curled up beneath the rack.

"Hey! There's a dog in here," she said to James. The dog had a squat, rectangular body, with a short dense coat and stocky legs. "It looks like a corgi."

"You're kidding . . ." said James, looking over her shoulder, then: "No, you're not. And it *is* a corgi. Where did he come from?"

Mandy shrugged. "I don't know."

Gran came to see what was going on. "A stowaway! We're going to have to retrace our footsteps to find the owner."

Mandy called to the dog. "Wake up, corgi! It's time to go home."

There was no response.

"He's very still," said James.

The corgi *was* still, abnormally still. Dogs didn't usually sleep that soundly, especially when people were moving around nearby and talking.

Mandy clapped her hands to get the corgi's attention. He didn't move. With a sinking heart, she clambered into the van and picked him up. "Oh, no! He's unconscious!" she gasped.

ABOUT THE AUTHOR

Ben M. Baglio was born in New York, and grew up in a small town in southern New Jersey. He was the only boy in a family with three sisters.

Ben spent a lot of his childhood reading. English was always his favorite subject, and after graduating from high school, he went on to study English Literature at the University of Pennsylvania. During his coursework, he was able to spend a year in Edinburgh, Scotland.

After graduation, Ben worked as a children's book editor in New York City. He also wrote his first book, which was about the Olympics in ancient Greece. Five years later, he took a job at a publishing house in England.

Ben is the author of the Dolphin Diaries series and is perhaps most well known for the Animal Ark and Animal Ark Hauntings series. These books were originally published in England (under the pseudonym Lucy Daniels) and have since gone on to be published in the U.S. and translated into fifteen languages.

Aside from writing, Ben enjoys scuba diving and swimming, music, and movies. He has a beagle named Bob, who is by his side whenever he writes.